SHANE PEACOCK

DOUBLE YOU

ORCA BOOK PUBLISHERS

Library and Archives Canada Cataloguing in Publication

Peacock, Shane, author
Double you / Shane Peacock.
(The seven sequels)

Issued in print and electronic formats.
ISBN 978-1-4598-0534-7 (pbk.).—ISBN 978-1-4598-0535-4 (pdf).—
ISBN 978-1-4598-0536-1 (epub)

I. Title.
PS8581.E234D68 2014   jc813'.54   c2014-901547-x
c2014-901548-8

First published in the United States, 2014
Library of Congress Control Number: 2014935388

Summary: Adam travels to Bermuda, Jamaica and New York in search of the truth
about his grandfather.

MIX
Paper from
responsible sources
FSC® C016245
www.fsc.org

*Orca Book Publishers is dedicated to preserving the environment and has
printed this book on Forest Stewardship Council® certified paper.*

Orca Book Publishers gratefully acknowledges the support for its publishing
programs provided by the following agencies: the Government of Canada
through the Canada Book Fund and the Canada Council for the Arts,
and the Province of British Columbia through the BC Arts Council
and the Book Publishing Tax Credit.

Design by Chantal Gabriell
Cover photography by Getty Images, Dreamstime, iStock, and CGTextures
Author photo by Kevin Kelly

ORCA BOOK PUBLISHERS   ORCA BOOK PUBLISHERS
PO Box 5626, Stn. B   PO Box 468
Victoria, BC Canada   Custer, WA USA
V8R 6S4   98240-0468

www.orcabook.com
Printed and bound in Canada.

17 16 15 14 • 4 3 2 1 ·

To Watson Peacock, a blunt instrument,
but loyal and true. R.I.P.

DAVID McLEAN
Greatest Grandpa
EVER?
Spy?
Or traitor?

ANN

DEBORAH

DJ

STEVE

SPENCER

BUNNY

ERIC WALTERS
SLEEPER

Driving a Jag
around London

JOHN WILSON
BROKEN ARROW

Sunshine and
sabotage in
Spain!

TED STAUNTON
CODA

Searching for
Bunny....

RICHARD SCRIMG
**THE WOL
AND ME**

Skating
home

MELANIE COLE

VERA McLEAN

CHARLOTTE   VICTORIA   SUZANNE

WEBB

ADAM

RENNIE

SIGMUND BROUWER
TIN SOLDIER

SHANE PEACOCK
DOUBLE YOU

NORAH McCLINTOCK
FROM THE DEAD

On the road in
the Deep South

Channeling
James Bond

Nazi-hunting
in Detroit

READ THE ORIGINAL
SEVEN (THE SERIES)

www.seventheseries.com

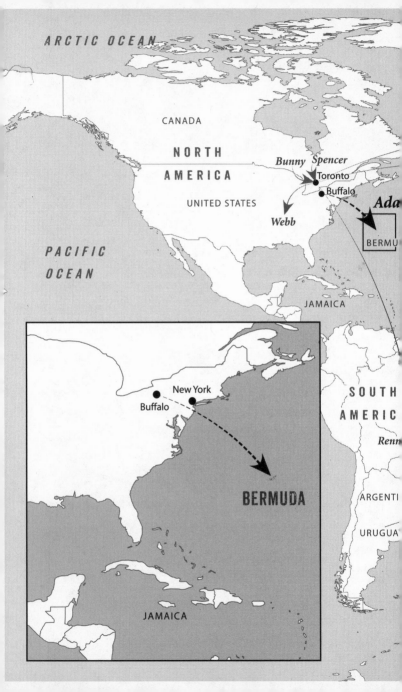

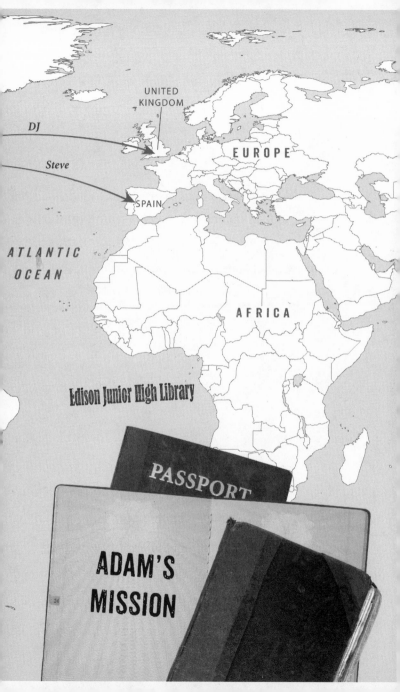

There's two sides to everyone.

—JOHN LE CARRÉ, *TINKER TAILOR SOLDIER SPY*

I never seen nobody but lied, one time or another.

—MARK TWAIN, *ADVENTURES OF HUCKLEBERRY FINN*

ONE

GUN

James Bond's weapon of choice is a Walther PPK pistol. You see it in his movies—a cold, hard piece of steel held in the grip of the most daring secret agent of all time. Sometimes it looks deceptively small, like an extension of his hand, while other times it's long and deadly, with a silencer attached to muffle the sound as another villain eats lead.

But now I was seeing it somewhere else, somewhere it didn't belong. It lay on a table in front of me at our family's cottage in northern Ontario, looking as innocent as a gun could—a gun used by a man with a license to kill. That man, of course, was 007, not my grandfather, David McLean, though within days I would begin to wonder if that description fit him too.

The gun mesmerized me. And when the others weren't looking, I took it. I even convinced myself that I hadn't *really* taken the gun *from* anyone, and certainly not to be used as a weapon. I reasoned, so far as I reasoned at all, that it didn't belong to anyone anymore and that I had no intention of using it (which is why it shocked me so much when I later employed it with such precision). I also told myself that I had every intention of giving it back (which I did) and that none of my cousins seemed to want it anyway.

Something consumed me when I saw it, something bad.

Bad Adam. I used to be him. He isn't dead or anything—I haven't completely killed him off. Now he lives inside me. He talks to me every now and then. He asks me to do things I know I shouldn't. Bad Adam is the guy who used to be insecure, who used to be mean to his amazing girlfriend, Shirley, who used to pine for a shallow but really attractive girl named Vanessa, who he liked just because of the way she looked. Bad Adam is also the guy who went on a trip to France last summer and acted like your typical "ugly American" almost from the minute he touched down. And, much to my shame, Bad Adam was also the one who hadn't really liked Grandpa very much for a long time. But that isn't me anymore.

On the day I first saw the Walther PPK, though, I was having a pretty hard time liking my grandfather. And I think most of my cousins felt the same way. I was trying, but the evidence against him was stacking up mighty fast.

We had all agreed to meet at the cottage that December day. Well, all of us except Rennie, who was in Uruguay, of all places, and Steve, who was in search of a little romance in Spain. So, five of the seven McLean grandsons were ready to spend a week or so together to finish off the holidays. In the old days, I would have despised that, but I was looking forward to reconnecting with the guys, seeing what it would be like to not be a jerk around them for once. It was the 26th, Boxing Day, and typically cold, typically Canadian.

Actually, that isn't fair, because Buffalo, New York, where I live, is just as cold as northern Ontario, maybe colder.

I had driven up with Webb. I think there were things going on in his family that he wasn't talking about. His stepfather had seemed like a bit of a bad dude, even worse than Bad Adam. I hadn't ever thought about Webb's problems before. But from the minute I really tried to connect with him, I could tell that he'd been through some tough times. You could see it in his eyes. I'd been texting him (in fact, I'd been texting and emailing all my cousins a lot since I'd come back from France), and he hadn't responded too often. And when the call came through from DJ about getting together—DJ, who is so full of himself and the supposed leader of our...wait, that's Bad Adam again. DJ is a good guy, actually. He looks out for the rest of us all he can.

Anyway, when he called to suggest we all get together at the cottage right after Christmas, I thought I'd reach out to Webb. I'm seventeen now, fully licensed (to drive, not to kill, though Mom might say that's one and the same thing with me), so I asked Webb if he'd like me to pick him up in Toronto. It took half a day for him to respond. And all he texted then was OK. I thought I'd wine and dine him a little to loosen him up, so I decided to take him to an IMAX film on the way up—pay the whole freight, the popcorn and everything. I was hoping we could see a real guys' flick, something with people just beating the crap out of each other. I figured we'd have a great time. Maybe Webb would even smile once. And it turned out that we were in luck. *Skyfall*, the latest James Bond movie, just happened to be on, fifty feet tall in IMAX! Man, I'd seen it at regular size a couple of times, and it had just blown me away, so I could hardly imagine what this would be like. Daniel Craig is sick, especially when he takes people out. Best Bond ever, and I know something about Bond. What guy (or girl—Craig walks around with his shirt off all the time) doesn't? But partway through the show, my reaction kind of worried me. I was pretty hyped up as I watched, especially during the scenes at the end where 007 wipes out Javier Bardem and every last one of his evil army of thugs in ammunition-packed action, and when Craig gets alone with the absolutely smokin' Bond Girl…and I started wondering if that was Bad Adam responding. Was I acting like what many people believe is typically American, getting off on gunplay and money and cars and perfect bodies and stuff? Vanessa would be into that kind of thing. (My girlfriend, Shirley, wouldn't.) For some reason, I started thinking about that shooting in Newtown, Connecticut, where that guy went into that school with an assault rifle and shot all those little kids. In seconds I was feeling really bad about enjoying the violence playing out on the screen. So I tried to cool it. But it was hard to do. It was James Bond, after all, the best Bond ever.

I don't remember much about driving up north. Webb didn't say a lot, even though I tried to get a conversation going. So it was mostly a blur. By the time we got to the cottage, DJ, Spencer and Bunny were gathered around a hole in the wall by the fireplace, their eyes nearly popping out of their heads. There was usually a lot of chopped wood piled up there, but since Grandpa's death it had dwindled. Spencer had pulled at the last log, really yanking and tearing at it, and it turned out to be nailed to a panel. When the panel came loose, things got really weird. Behind it was a sort of secret chamber! A bunch of stuff fell out: a leather bag, a sack of golf balls with strange letters on them, and all kinds of cash, in different denominations from all over the world. And the Walther PPK, of course, which I couldn't stop staring at, though I think I hid my interest pretty well. Then DJ found some passports sewn into the lining of the bag. They came from different countries and had Grandpa's picture on every one, but none of the names was David McLean! We were all speechless. It was pretty freaky—scary and exciting and upsetting at the same time.

I felt like I was having an out-of-body experience. I could hear the guys talking almost as if they were in the distance. Suddenly, I was worried that I knew *exactly* what my grandfather was, and he wasn't anything like any of us had ever imagined. Fake passports, all those foreign bills, that particular gun.

"It's pretty," said Bunny about the cash. "It looks like Monopoly money."

Bunny has some learning problems, and I used to think he was a family embarrassment. But he's actually pretty cool, a great guy with an interesting rather than weak mind. If you really listen to him, he always tells the truth—about everything. We studied a Shakespeare play in school called *King Lear* and there was a character in it called the Fool. He was the smartest guy in the story, but you had to really pay attention to know that. In real life—in *my* life—that's our Bunny.

"This stuff is for real," muttered Webb. The things we were looking at were so mind-blowing that even he was coming to life.

They started counting the money and speculating about what it all meant. I was trying to look calm and normal. I said something about Grandpa maybe just liking to keep some cash on hand. But this was piles and piles of cash, not a few extra bucks, so it was a pretty lame thing to say. I was desperate to find reasons for Grandpa hiding this stash. The things he had asked me to do in France this past summer had turned around my life. He had made me look into myself and see what was important: the good in me, the good we all have inside us. He had made me into a better person—into Good Adam. He couldn't be a bad guy. He couldn't! It felt like my life depended on it.

The guys turned to the gun. And Spencer took the words right out of my mind.

"It's not just a gun," he said. "This is a Walther PPK."

For some reason, I pretended I didn't already know that. Spencer, who is a pretty bright guy in a kind of eccentric way—funny and witty—really knows his movies. He wants to direct them—he already does, in fact—so he knew exactly what that gun was and exactly who had used it on the screen.

Spencer worried me because I had the feeling he was going to jump on the same idea that was percolating in my mind—these hidden materials were the tools of a spy. I knew Spence could make a pretty good case for it. I just hoped he would be conjuring a David McLean who was like James Bond, a good guy always doing what was right. But I knew better than to think that way.

Since I'd come back from France, I'd been reforming myself in more ways than one. I was trying to treat others better, especially Shirley, and I was rebuilding myself too, both body and soul. I worked out all the time and had begun studying a martial art that I'd read Robert Downey Jr. did, a rather vicious but effective form of self-defense called Wing Chun. I worked hard at it and was getting pretty good. It actually taught you how to relax and expand your mind too, even while you were in combat. But I was also trying much harder at school and doing a lot of reading, which I hadn't been so big on before. I'd stopped playing so many video games and stopped reading trashy books. Some of the better novels I'd read were about espionage, and a couple were by this guy named John Le Carré. One was called *The Spy Who Came in from the Cold* and the other was called *Tinker Tailor Soldier Spy*. They were hard going, with kind of boring, intricate prose and complicated, sometimes hard-to-follow ideas, but I stuck with them. Le Carré wrote about what spies were really like. And they weren't like James Bond. They were ordinary people with suspicious minds and dirty tactics. Their whole world was dirty. And lots of them, *lots* of them, were traitors and double agents.

Go, Spencer, I thought. Convince us that David McLean was a hero like James Bond. Bad Adam, of course, was telling me that Grandpa wasn't a hero, that chances were, he was awfully sketchy, like most spies. And in minutes, Bad Adam's argument was backed up by some awfully strong evidence.

"If I had to hazard a guess," said Spencer, "I'd say Grandpa was a—"

"He wasn't a spy," snapped DJ.

You tell him, my serious, decent, big cousin, I thought.

But then DJ ruined his own argument. I had been poking around more in the chamber in the wall, hoping the other guys wouldn't notice, and I found a black notebook way at the back. I was worried about what was in it and wanted to keep a grip on it. But DJ asked for it as soon as he saw it, and when DJ asks for something, you give it to him. He opened the notebook and started reading aloud. "*I hoped I'd never have to use this book,*" he began, "*but I needed to keep my own record, my own account, in case things ever came tumbling down around me.*" That sounded awfully defensive, as if Grandpa was making excuses for something bad he'd done in the past. "*I just know that I always did what needed to be done. Nothing more and nothing less.*"

I looked down at the Walther PPK, and my spirits kept sinking.

DJ started flipping through the pages. I was right next to him and could see what was on them.

There were all sorts of drawings and numbers and strange, incomplete sentences that didn't make any sense, all in Grandpa's handwriting.

Then it got even worse.

As DJ leafed through the pages, an envelope fell out. I picked it up quickly and considered hiding it. But the other guys had already seen it. I held it out for them to look at it. Everyone moved in closer. It was just an old envelope; the letter inside was gone. Addressed to my grandfather, it had a return address in Bermuda on it, and you could see a few words embedded into the surface of the envelope, as if the writer was so angry when he wrote the letter that he had pressed down on his pen really hard, engraving the words into the envelope beneath the paper. I held it up to the light and, stupidly, because I was so anxious to see what it said, read out loud, "*You are a traitor. You deserve to die.*" The second the words were out of my mouth, I clammed up. I felt like a traitor myself. I shoved the envelope into my pocket.

"Still think he wasn't a spy?" asked Spencer, smiling at DJ. Spence almost seemed to be enjoying this. He was way too into the movies.

"Maybe he was, but he wasn't a traitor!" shouted my usually calm big cousin. It was an interesting choice of words, given what we had all just read. His reaction reminded me of a line from *Hamlet*, something about *The lady doth protest too much.*

DJ was no lady. He was a big, strapping athlete who could run over you like a train on the football field, but he was definitely protesting too much. Our teacher had explained what that line meant: sometimes people say things and actually mean the opposite. Even DJ was seriously worried about our hero now.

And then Bunny fired the gun. And I made my move.

The sound was like a cannon exploding right next to us. It was awesome. (At least, that was what Bad Adam thought.) As soon as we picked ourselves up off the floor, Spencer (who is great at looking out for his brother) asked for big, bad Bunny's weapon. The Bun-Man, of course, pointed it straight at him as he offered it. Spencer ducked…and I reached out and took the gun. It was almost sleight of hand: I passed it behind my back and slipped it into my pocket, and no one noticed. They were arguing, loudly, not looking at me. I didn't say a word. I stood there with my heart pounding. One thought was coursing through my brain: Grandpa kept a loaded gun at the cottage!

"Could everybody just be quiet?" yelled DJ.

He started taking control, like he usually does. He had figured out that there were twelve passports and twelve sections in the notebook, each with a crudely drawn flag that seemed to associate it with a particular country: England, Spain, Russia, Argentina, etc. He reasoned that with my dad working, Spence and Bunny's dad out of town and our moms on a Caribbean cruise together, we could actually take the cash and the passports and the evidence in the notebooks and find out what Grandpa was up to. All we had to do was be back home by New Year's Eve. It would be amazing!

At first it seemed kind of crazy to me, but I'd been on my own in France earlier that year, and I'd flown alone to California and back to visit a cousin on Dad's side a month ago. All I needed was a day or two to check out the address on the envelope. A couple quick flights and home. And we couldn't keep the money anyway. We'd have to explain it, and that might incriminate my grandfather. We almost had to spend it. I had to know about Grandpa too. I had to.

Everyone chose a country. I was assigned the job of passing the Argentine stuff on to Rennie in South America. DJ made it sound as if we were about to find out all the brave and marvelous things good old Grandpa had done, as if it were a James Bond movie.

One part of me hoped he was right. But the other part feared the worst.

And so that was how I found myself flying into the beautiful island of Bermuda the very next day, a John Le Carré novel in hand, fear in my belly and a Walther PPK pistol in my luggage. Bad Adam was thrilled.

TWO

FANTASY ISLAND

We'd all made a beeline out of northern Ontario the minute we decided we were going to investigate this big question mark in Grandpa's past. I think I moved the fastest. We had six days, including Boxing Day. So really, we only had five. That was it. In five days, I had to find the truth about David McLean. If that truth was horrible, which I suspected it was, I didn't know what I was going to do. It could very well ruin many lives, especially mine.

I'd taken the bullets out of the clip in the Walther PPK back in Canada and just left the unloaded gun in my luggage when I crossed the border. So it wasn't really a weapon now, just my grandfather's empty keepsake. In fact, I had found a small document at the cottage calling the gun a "collectible." I'd brought that with me too. Still, I was pretty tense. Thank goodness, I went through without an inspection.

Maybe I shouldn't have been bringing it with me at all, but I knew it was part of the puzzle I was trying to solve. If I brought it to the address on the envelope, it might somehow answer some questions. Also, for some reason, I just couldn't leave it behind.

The house had been empty when I got back to Buffalo. I love being alone when my parents aren't around. Lots of things to do, things they might not let me do if they were home. Bad Adam really loves it. But I hadn't had a minute to waste. I'd wanted to take a really early flight (one that left at about five in the morning, or, as I imagine they say in the secret service, zero five hundred hours) to New York. I'd thrown some clothes into a small bag—no fuss; just get in, find the information and get out of Bermuda fast. I had to be realistic. That's all I could handle. I'd grabbed the Le Carré novel and the American Airlines annual pass Dad had given me for the trip to France. All the pilots can get them, and he's one of the best in the airline, the one and only Captain John Murphy, a decorated Gulf War hero whose calm and expertise have saved lives in a few hairy situations. I'm proud of him. Bad Adam resents him sometimes, but not me.

I'd texted my cousin Rennie and gotten him up to speed on everything. He'd written back immediately, intrigued by what I'd told him and especially curious about the Argentine passport and accompanying newspaper clippings among Grandpa's things. He'd asked if I could scan the stuff, along with relevant pages from the notebook. So I'd emailed it all to him in South America and wondered what in the world he'd discover down there. But that was his deal—I didn't have a minute to even think about it.

The pilot's pass gets you get through airline customs really quickly. They hardly even look at your bags. Dad says the best thing to do at an airport is to always tell the truth, even if the truth is a bit outrageous. So I told them when I checked in that I had something in my stowed luggage that I thought they needed to approve. Although I don't think he's ever used it, Dad has a hard-shell metal carrying case, which is what's required for transporting a small firearm on a plane. That's the law. I had put the PPK in it and then placed it in my bag. I also had the document saying that it was a collectible and that its firing pin had been removed. I knew that wasn't true, since Bunny had actually fired the gun back at the cottage, but it was just a tiny lie, a harmless one too. Grandpa had had all the appropriate papers but had kept this thing loaded. Why? From what or from whom did he feel he needed protection? My heart was absolutely pounding when I opened my luggage for inspection. It was James Bond's gun, and it had a deadly look to it. I took a deep breath.

"I have an unloaded weapon in here," I told the man at the special-baggage check. He was of East Indian heritage, kind of old, wearing a white turban and sporting a pretty cool beard and shades like a shady character in a movie. I supposed it helped him hide the emotion in his eyes. Another employee, a bit younger but almost identical, was standing nearby, and so was a young woman, East Indian too, wearing black pants, white shirt, a tie and badges. She had beautiful long hair, raven-black like her eyes, and wore a fair bit of makeup. It looked like she had shrunk her uniform to make it more form fitting. And her form, Bad Adam noticed, was pretty awesome.

"I am going to take it out now," I said. "It's just a show model, a collectible; the firing pin has been removed. I have the documents." I gave the paper to him. "I'll take it out and hand it to you, butt first. My father is Captain John Murphy. You have his pilot's ID." I'd brought the copy Dad kept at home in his desk. I'd already given them the pass.

"Step away from the luggage, sir," the old guy said quickly. He had a strong accent, but I got what he said, loud and clear. "Stand back behind that line, please. I will do this."

I stood back, my heart racing. Why had I brought the gun?

His eyes still on me, he approached the bag very slowly, as if a bomb were in it. I felt like making a joke about it, but wisely kept my mouth shut. He continued to stare at me, reaching blindly for the case, feeling around for it. When he found it, he kept eyeballing me. It was almost funny. But I didn't laugh. I'd left the gun case on top on purpose, so he found it quickly. Slowly, ever so slowly, he pulled it from the bag. He snapped open the case and took it out. It glistened under the terminal's bright lights. He turned his attention from me to it, as if he couldn't resist. His eyes glowed, and he seemed to forget about me for an instant.

"It's a Walther PPK," he said quietly, in admiration.

"James Bond?" said the younger man, peering over the older guy's shoulder, his mouth open, staring at the weapon.

"Daniel Craig." The young woman grinned.

The old guy's smile vanished.

"What is the meaning of this?" he demanded, glaring at me.

"It's just a—"

He hadn't looked at the documents I'd given him. The sight of the gun had thrown him.

"Can I hold it?" asked the younger man.

"Ladies first," said the woman, reaching out.

"No one will hold it!" snapped the old guy. "Not even this young man. He is going straight back to—"

"Mr. Petal, may I speak with you for a moment?" said the younger guy.

They all stepped aside, the old guy still holding the PPK. It was like he wanted to keep it. They started whispering. I heard just a few bits of their conversation, as the younger man and woman made their case. I had a pilot's pass, they said, from a pilot with pedigree; the gun wasn't loaded; the boy had been up-front. It wasn't illegal to transport a gun, especially an unloaded collectible with papers, placed in a proper container. "We could give him a permit." They didn't bother to check the firing pin.

About an hour later (zero ten hundred hours), after filling out all sorts of forms, I was on the plane and so was my pistol. I had a permit to take it to Bermuda and bring it back. I also had the empty envelope on my lap, with the address on the island written clearly across the front.

I used to be a nervous flyer, which I'd never told Grandpa because I thought he might be ashamed of me. (This was a guy, after all, who had been shot down over enemy-occupied Europe in the war.) But with his guidance I got over my fear when I went to France. So on this trip, I loved being in the air. I loved staring down at the world below. It was funny how it was so cold in New York and seemed so cold outside while we headed out over the Atlantic, but about an hour and a half later, when Bermuda came into view, everything looked warm.

From the air, Bermuda looks like a giant fish hook, a fish hook for the rich. Or maybe it's more like the head of a thin dinosaur with its mouth open. Whatever it is, it's pretty amazing, sitting there way out in the Atlantic Ocean, green even in late December, surrounded by sandy beaches and incredible blue water.

We came in over the eastern tip of the island. I could see the single runway of the airport below. It seemed like everything else was covered with a green carpet; there were many golf courses and parks set off by startlingly colorful houses—purple and pink and yellow—all with shining white roofs. There were boats everywhere too, gathered in the turquoise waves off the island's shores—everything from sailboats to motorboats and yachts to cruise ships. They looked like baby birds flocking close to their mother. People were walking around in shirtsleeves.

It was early afternoon, about thirteen hundred hours.

My pass got me through customs and onto the street quickly. I walked out into an almost perfect day, about like late spring in Buffalo, maybe even early summer. It was cloudy, but the sun poked through every now and then. Palm trees above me cast shadows on the wide sidewalk and out over the pickup lanes at the arrivals area. I pulled my shades over my eyes, looked up and down a line of cabs and motioned for one. As I waited, I checked out everyone who passed. Bad Adam eyed the women, dressed in summer clothes. A bearded Bermudian with long Rasta hair, wearing long camo shorts, a colorful yellow-and-red shirt and a porkpie hat, leaped out of a taxi and approached me with a smile.

"That is all your baggage, sir?" he asked.

"That's right," I said. My plan was to say little to anyone. But he was a smiler and a talker.

"Not want to stay on the beautiful island long, sir?"

He had a bit of what sounded to me like a Jamaican accent, but it was British too—more British than anything, in fact. Whatever it was, it sounded relaxed and gentle.

"No." I didn't look at him. And I didn't offer him the bag. I was keeping it with me. I was wearing long pants and my hard black boots, a *Skyfall* T-shirt and a jean jacket. I liked the fact that I was tall and, especially with my shades on, could probably pass for a few years older than I was, maybe even twenty or twenty-one. That might come in handy here, all alone. I'd shoved the envelope into a pocket, deep down so no one could see it. I simply got into the backseat and closed the door.

"Whatever you like, man," he said to me through the open window. He looked a little disappointed.

When he got back in, I gave him the address. I didn't take the envelope out at all. In fact, I'd considered burning it or leaving it at home. But it was the only lead I had.

"That is in Paget Parish," he said, turning to look at me with a big smile.

"I wasn't aware of that."

"Well, it is. Nice area, not too far from Hamilton, the BEEG city here." He laughed loudly. I didn't. "Right," he said. "To Paget."

We headed out of the airport and across an amazing causeway, a thin needle of road connecting the airport to the rest of Bermuda. That's all it was: a highway right out across the water. From the side it looked like it was made of stone, but when you were on it, it was just a modern, smooth highway with short concrete walls on either side.

"Shall I give you the tour, sir?"

"No."

"Just a short one?"

"No, thank you."

"We have many things of interest here. Do you like caves?"

My heart gave a quick beat. *Caves?* Why would he say that?

"We have the world's greatest, most beautiful crystalline caves."

"I…I'm not into caves." That was a lie. I'd been in the world's most awesome cave in France. And it had changed my life.

"How about—?"

"I'm just here for part of a day," I said quickly. I hadn't even booked a hotel. My airline pass was open—I could leave whenever I wanted.

He seemed disappointed again.

We crossed over onto land, and then the road curved toward the ocean. We moved along the beautiful blue water under palm trees mixed with other coniferous trees that looked just like something you might see in northern Ontario. It was a strange combination. I was wondering if they'd imported the palm trees. That would be just like the Brits. I'd read a bit about Bermuda in some of the tourist material on the airplane. Main facts: about 65,000 people on a small island, lots of golf courses, colorful houses, rich people, great shopping, nice beaches and loads of sightseeing for tourists—loads of tourists period, even in December. The British had run the place for a long time, even though now there was a real mosaic of races. As I looked out the window, everything I'd read was confirmed. Rich people in luxury cars, stunning fairways, beautiful beaches with a few people on them…and a driver who liked to drive slowly and talk a lot. Folks here were supposed to be friendly. I'd become a friendly guy myself. But today I had a mission, and I had to get it done. Grandpa's reputation depended on it.

"Do you like history, my friend?"

"Yes."

"Yes?" He seemed relieved—and excited.

"Shall I share some history of the island for you as we drive along in this paradise?"

"Yeah…sure."

He began by telling me that Bermuda had been uninhabited for a long time, and then the British came in the seventeenth century and set up tobacco farms. They brought slaves to work on the farms, and later on tourists started to vacation on the island, Americans brought their influences, and then there were the spies—

"Excuse me?" I asked, stopping him in mid-sentence.

"Yes, man?"

"Spies?"

"During the Second World War, sir. Bermuda was an important place then. We had spies all over. They say the Princess Hotel, the beautiful pink hotel in Hamilton, was filled with them, intercepting the mail that came through our lovely island from Nazi Germany, reading it all, looking for invisible ink messages and microdots on letters and full sentences on the heads of pins, sir. They say many important spies lived here."

"Which ones?"

"If I knew that, sir, then I would know what no one knows."

"Huh?" When I said that, I thought of my Canadian cousins, who make fun of me when I say it, especially if I bring up the fact that they say "Eh?" all the time (which they do). They like to respond with, "It's better than HUH?" and make it sound like I'm a hillbilly or something. They're such cards. Bunny says "huh" about a thousand times a day when I'm around.

"I mean that the spies in Bermuda were very secretive," continued my driver. "No one like James Bond was here, my friend."

"Huh?"

"Real spies"—he turned to me and lowered his voice— "are invisible. They assume the color of the wall. They aren't famous; they don't carry guns. They just eliminate people, or have someone else do it for them." Then he laughed out loud again. "I don't know, sir. I don't have a clue about spies! But I heard a particularly famous one lived in Paget."

"A famous one?"

"Yes, sir. He was a Canadian. Imagine that! Canadians would make perfect spies. I've met a few of them, you know. Boring, but full of secrets!

They are kind of like icebergs." He laughed. This guy just loved to laugh.

"Canadian, eh?"

He laughed again before I realized what I'd said.

"That's what I've heard anyway. This man was a very powerful person. But who knows?" He sighed. "Yes, indeed. Apparently, he had a very common name."

"Like Bill or Bob."

"Yes."

"Or maybe...Dave?"

"Could have been. Here, we are approaching Hamilton."

I could see the town—almost a city—getting closer. The number of buildings had been increasing, going from just a few hotels, resort-type restaurants and shops to many, some with a slightly more urban feel. Hamilton looked old and quaint and also had some buildings more than a few stories high. But we turned at a busy traffic circle (lots of those in Bermuda) and headed left, away from the town. It was countryside, but residential at the same time.

"We are now entering Paget. What was the address again?"

I gave it to him.

"Interesting."

"Why?"

"I think that house is secluded."

"Secluded?"

"And that is unusual in Paget."

We were soon off the main road, making our way through streets with tightly spaced houses and then into an area where none were close together. I figured that most people here had enough money to be separated a bit from each other. Everyone seemed to have a good-sized lawn. But then there was a gap of several empty properties. We had gone along some rather hilly streets, and now my driver turned and went up a pretty steep one, with no houses on either side for about a couple hundred yards. He stopped at a gate with high walls. I could see a nearly white house up the hill, different because of its lack of color. The iron gate looked like the letter *W*. It almost seemed like it had been designed that way.

My driver blew a low, admiring whistle as he got out and walked around to my window.

"This is quite the place. Who are you?" he asked, smiling. "An important man?"

"I'm no one," I said quickly. It sounded stupid as soon as I said it.

"No one?"

"Just a Canadian...tourist," I lied. I wasn't sure why I did that. Maybe it was Bad Adam talking.

"Ah, a Canadian! I should have guessed. Lots of secrets...eh?" He gave another one of his huge laughs. "Well, Mr. No One, we apparently must ring this bell here to even get onto the property. Is this the King of Canada's holiday home?" He pressed the button on the gate.

"Just a friend."

"Friend?"

"Hello?" demanded a gruff voice coming over the intercom speaker on the gate.

"Yes, man, this is Emmanuel Robb, taxi driver extraordinaire for Island Cabs, and I have a passenger here for you by the name of—" He turned to me.

"McLean," I said. "Adam McLean." It was just a small lie.

Emmanuel turned back to the speaker. "McLean," he said dramatically. "Adam McLean." Then he paused and added, "From Canada."

"Just a moment," said the voice. "Stay there." He said it like an order.

We must have waited for ten minutes. I stayed in the cab, Emmanuel leaning through the window, regaling me with Bermudian stories. It was actually getting hot. Finally, the intercom crackled.

"Hello?" said the gruff voice over the speaker, startling us.

Emmanuel rushed back up to the gate.

"Yes?"

"We have a question for Mr. McLean."

I got out of the cab and approached.

"Yes?" I asked.

"Are you any relation to David?"

THREE

MR. KNOW

It was very weird. When I told the voice on the intercom that I was David McLean's grandson, the doors began opening, almost as if some big boss was listening and had pressed an open sesame button the instant the words were out of my mouth. Whoever this person was, he or she was anxious to see me.

"Walk up," the speaker said. "Leave the cab at the gate and walk up. Mr. Robb, you may be on your way. Mr. McLean, pay your man and send him off. We can see you from where we are." I was so lame at this game, I hadn't even noticed the camera peering down at us from the top of the gate. "You must enter alone.

Come to the front door and I will await you there."
He had a Bermudian accent too, though a little more
refined than Emmanuel's.

It was a long steep walk. The lawn was well kept
but not perfect. A rich guy lived here, somebody who
was pretty comfortable but not a multimillionaire.
Comfortable enough to have a servant or a security guy. The driveway curved in front of the house,
and as I walked along beside a hedge that hid the
front doors and the windows, I could see someone,
a big someone, standing on the white stone steps at
the entrance. He was wearing a cream-colored suit,
no tie, and I thought I could see a bulge under his
jacket, right where a gun holster would be. I thought
of the Walther PPK in my bag and wondered if
I should have brought the bullets. He had close-
cropped blond hair and shades so dark that I couldn't
see his eyes move behind them.

"Mr. McLean?" he asked.

No, Daniel Craig, I thought, here to kick your ass.
Bad Adam again. Who did he think I was though? He'd
seen me on his surveillance camera. But he was awfully
serious, and I supposed people in his line of work,
whatever line that was, had to be sure of everything.

"Yes."

"You may enter."

How kind of you, thought Bad Adam. "Thank you," I said.

It was very quiet inside. A clock was ticking somewhere and it sounded really loud. The house appeared to be all on one level, but large and sprawling; a series of huge picture windows lined the far end of the house. From the front door you could see a big living room and dining area with all sorts of comfortable leather sofas and chairs, expensive-looking art on the walls and sculptures on antique wooden tables. Though the walls were white, every piece of furniture was dark. There were lots of photographs, too, all black and white, of famous leaders from the past—guys like President John F. Kennedy and the famous Cuban dictator Fidel Castro and even Nikita Khrushchev, the Soviet Union communist boss in the 1950s and '60s. There were closed doors leading out of the open area, giving the impression that the house hid a warren of secret chambers.

We were up on a hill, so the view was amazing—the city of Hamilton in the distance with its colorful buildings and white roofs, green palm trees and the peacock-blue Atlantic Ocean beyond. In the fore-ground I could see a swimming pool. Lounging on one of the chairs and reading was a girl. She could have been anywhere from sixteen to twenty (it's hard to tell girls' ages sometimes). Bad Adam was disappointed that she was wearing baggy sweatpants and a baggy sweatshirt, gray on gray. He was trying to check her out. She had medium-length reddish-brown hair, uncombed and hanging over her face. She was wearing shades and a black New York Yankees ballcap. She peered through the window at me. In fact, she got up and looked in. But I had to pay attention to my brawny guide.

"Stay there," he said, pointing to a spot on the floor. He seemed to like that phrase. He turned and knocked on a door. It opened and another man came out—similar build, similar suit, similar bulge in his jacket, though this guy was black. They whispered to each other and then the white guy disappeared through the door, closing it behind him, and the black guy walked into the living room.

"This way, Mr. McLean," he said in a smooth Bermudian accent, motioning for me to sit on one of the leather sofas.

What were these guys, mobsters? I wondered what in the world I'd walked into.

Half an hour later, we were both still sitting there in silence. He never smiled, even though I gave him a few friendly looks. The magazines on the table were pretty unusual. There were a few about present-day Bermuda (and there was a local newspaper), but most of them were from the 1960s—*Time* and one called *Newsweek*. I picked up a few and leafed through them; lots of stories about long-dead people.

The girl, who I had noticed was looking at me every now and then, eventually got up, slid open one of the floor-to-ceiling glass doors and approached us, her bare feet gently slapping on the cool stone floor.

"Hello, Jim," she said to the black guy. Her accent was pretty spectacular. A girl with those gentle Bermudian tones. Pretty cool.

"Angel," he said in a monotone.

"Where's John?"

"He went to get Mr. No."

Went to get him? I thought. Where was he, in Timbuktu? It seemed like forever since John had left us.

"Mr. K-N-O-W?" she sneered. "Is that what we are calling him today?"

"Angel, behave."

"Oh, I know, play the game. Who's this?"

She motioned toward me, sliding her shades down. A slight girl, not very tall; seventeen, I thought, maybe even eighteen. *Nice eyes,* thought Bad Adam. They were blue like the ocean, but she covered them up quickly. *No stunner,* added Bad Adam to himself as he gave her a fuller examination. *Kind of mousy, but maybe with some potential.*

"This is Mr. McLean," said John.

I stood up to greet her. I believe in treating women with respect. I always open doors for Shirley. She deserves it, deserves to be thought of as someone special. Grandpa taught me that. "I'm pleased to meet you," I said and extended my hand.

"My, aren't we formal," said Angel as she turned and walked away. Two steps later she tripped over a stool and looked embarrassed. But she recovered, opened the sliding door, looked at me over her shoulder and went back outside. I had noticed the book in her hand. It was *The Human Factor* by Graham Greene. I'd heard about him. He was considered a great writer—pretty heavy—and he sometimes wrote about spies. It wasn't light reading. She must be smart, I thought in admiration. *Oh no, just my luck,* thought Bad Adam.

I glanced over at John for a reaction, but he simply looked straight back at me, shades still on. It was a little disconcerting.

An hour later, Jim appeared. My stomach had begun rumbling.

"Mr. Know is ready to receive you."

"Receive me?" I said and then wondered why I'd said it out loud.

"Yes, Mr. McLean. Come with us."

John walked in front of me and Jim behind. I could swear they moved their hands closer to the bulges in their suit coats. We headed through a big wooden door into what I thought was a bedroom but turned out to be a sort of office with surveillance monitors, then through another door and into another room, and then another. Each time, John would open the door, we'd all go through it, and then Jim would close the door behind us. The doors were so thick and tightly hung that when they closed, you heard absolutely no sound from beyond them, as if we were in soundproof chambers. Then we entered the last room. It was huge, also an office of some sort, but with no surveillance monitors. It had dark mahogany walls, black leather sofas and chairs, more black-and-white pictures on the walls and more sculptures. It, too, had a sense of being frozen in the 1960s. The ceiling was low, and there were no windows. A few lamps dimly lit the room. Jim and John brought me to a halt a good twenty feet from a big oak desk. It was spotless, polished to a shine. There was nothing on it except an eye, a glass eye sitting there alone like a raft on calm water. The iris in it was gold. An old man in a wheelchair sat behind the desk, his back turned to us.

"Mr. Know?" said John.

The old man slowly swung around in his chair and stared at me.

It was Grandpa.

FOUR

THE DAHL BUILDING

"I've waited for this moment for so long," said Grandpa. For some reason, he didn't sound happy. But it was *him*—his face, his voice, his expression. It was David McLean, my incredible grandfather!

I've never fainted before, but I almost did at that moment. I was immediately in tears, tears of joy, and I started feeling wobbly and weak. For a few seconds, I couldn't move, not a single muscle. I stood there stunned, immobile as a statue.

He was alive! I stared at him. It was impossible, absolutely, positively impossible. Hadn't my cousins and I seen him in his coffin? But there was no doubt that he was sitting right in front of me. I knew if I went to him, I could touch him. He even held his head slightly to the left, like he always did. Still, I couldn't believe it. Then I thought of what we had found at the cottage, all the evidence of the secrets he had kept from us, all those passports, the money, and the Walther PPK. If David McLean really *was* a spy, then MI6 or the CIA could have made this happen— they could make anything happen. In fact, they might do this sort of thing often. Maybe spies faked their own deaths all the time.

I rushed toward him. Two steps forward, then John and Jim seized me.

"Grandpa!" I cried. "Grandpa, how…you're…" I sputtered, and then I blurted out, "I…I love you! I'm sorry for the way I—"

"You love me?" he sneered.

"Yes! Of course I do! Let me GO!" I screamed at the two men. They were as strong as oxen.

"Well, I don't love you, my boy."

I froze.

"Love is unaffordable in this world, though I know I made it look as if I believed in it. I had a job to do, Adam. And I have one now. It is bigger than anything else in my world—in the world, period. Family must come second. Your mother and her sisters, you and your cousins, have their place. One must have priorities."

It was a phrase Grandpa often used, but he'd never used it like this.

"What do you mean? Why are you talking like this? Make them let me go!" I was ashamed of my tears, yet I couldn't stop them. But Grandpa almost seemed to enjoy my pain. He was smiling at me with exactly the same smile he'd used so many times when he talked to me in my childhood.

"There is more in this world than is dreamt of in your little mind."

He was paraphrasing Shakespeare, another line from *Hamlet*. Grandpa had always loved to quote from literature.

"What do you—?"

"You *cannot* know that I am alive, Adam. Neither can your mother or father or your cousins. It is unacceptable. Impossible."

"But you showed yourself to me."

"Nevertheless"—he gave me a hard look—"now I must eliminate you."

"Eliminate?" My stomach burned.

"Look at me."

I looked right into his eyes, those amazing blue eyes I had never dreamed I would see again. "Take him away," he said to his two thugs, still staring at me but with something hidden in his expression, something I couldn't place. Was he trying to tell me something? Signal me somehow? "Take him to the Dahl building and finish him. You know how. Adam, I am sorry I have to do this, but nevertheless…I do."

As Jim held me, John frisked me in a few quick motions, amazingly fast and professional. He felt my cell phone and ripped it out of my pocket. He flipped it to Grandpa, who opened a top drawer in his desk and set it inside, closing it immediately afterward.

"Bring me his other things. I'll put them in here too."

Then they pulled me screaming from the room. Grandpa watched as I was taken away. Once we'd reached the second soundproof room, they put thick tape over my mouth. I moaned and tried to wrestle free.

"Tell Angel to go to her room," said John to Jim. I had enough Wing Chun training to take out almost anyone, I thought, even a big guy, and I had put on lots of muscle recently, but John had pipes like a blacksmith and had me in a tight grip, locking my arms and holding me down. It hurt. He seemed to really know what he was doing. Jim exited and came back a few minutes later.

"Okay, let's move him."

They dragged me into the area by the front door. I looked down and saw my bag still sitting there, with the Walther PPK inside. All my cash and my passport were in there too. Though I kept trying to kick and wriggle my way out of their grips, they pulled me through the house to the glass doors and then across the big backyard. I could see a small building up ahead. It was made of unpainted steel. They unlocked it, threw me in and then slammed the door and secured it. I couldn't hear anything once I was inside. It was soundproof too. I tore off the tape, ripping out the hairs growing on my upper lip. It hurt like crazy. But I didn't give it a second thought. I shouted at the top of my lungs. It didn't matter. No one could hear me. I slumped down on the floor and cried. Grandpa was alive! He was alive but he was...I don't know... someone horrible and uncompromising, and unlike the man I had known…nothing like what he had always pretended to be! Then I thought of the stories Mom had told me about him constantly being away, flying around, running his "import/export" business. It had always seemed a bit mysterious, and he'd never said much about it. If he really was a spy or at least someone with big secrets, maybe he had no choice but to hide them. Maybe he *had* to eliminate me; maybe it was for the greater good. I didn't know. But why couldn't he find a way to *protect* me? Protect me no matter what? I collapsed and sobbed again.

But I didn't cry for long. The building was one very small room. You could stand in the middle and almost touch the sides. There were no lights, just long horizontal slits up high in the walls, about an inch or two wide and a foot long, where light came in through what appeared to be incredibly thick glass— soundproof too, no doubt. There was nothing in the building but a desk and a chair, some yellow writing pads, some pencils with erasers, and a few books. I was surprised to see that many of them were by Roald Dahl, the guy who wrote *Charlie and the Chocolate Factory, James and the Giant Peach* and *The BFG,* some of the most famous kids' books ever written.

I loved them when I was a kid, mostly because they all had an edge and also because Grandpa had read some of them to me. But why were they here in this prison he had put me in? That made no sense.

I sat there for hours, it seemed, many hours. No one brought food, nothing happened. It got darker, then completely black. I could barely see the nose on my face.

Then the walls began to move.

FIVE

CRUSHED

Two of the walls were moving inward.

It was barely detectable at first. They rumbled slowly toward me. Within minutes I would be crushed to death. *This* was how I was to be eliminated! There would be almost nothing left of me. They had a perfect plan.

At first, I just screamed. But I was screaming into a void. By great strength of will, I stopped and forced myself to think. Maybe this was a dream. I pinched myself—hard. It hurt. I slapped myself across the face. Really hurt. I was still in the little building, and the walls were still coming at me. I tried to keep from panicking.

"What would Grandpa do?" I asked out loud. It seemed like such a stupid question at first. Why would I want to do *anything* Grandpa did anymore? How could I look up to a single thing about him, anything he had ever said or done? But he had always been the guy with the ideas in our family, the one we'd all leaned on in a crisis.

So, I told myself, maybe I *should* think about what he'd do. Maybe my new lethal and dedicated grandfather was actually a good role model in this desperate situation. Evil or good, he got the job done. Grandpa had survived a lot: the Spanish Civil War, a plane crash in Iceland, the Nazis in occupied southern France, dangerous adventures in Africa. And those were just the things I knew about. He had likely remained cool through it all. Mom was like that too—calm under fire. Also, it was apparent now that Grandpa had lived a life of deception. He was like a guy in a John Le Carré novel. *What would he do?* Time was running out.

"I need to remain cool too," I said out loud as calmly as I could. "I need to think clearly."

I tried to find something or someone to calm me, but I didn't think of Shirley. Her kind face, more beautiful to me than anyone else's, wouldn't comfort me now; it would upset me, because I wanted to be with her and hold her in my arms. I thought instead of Leon Worth.

The walls kept closing in on me, terrifying me. I couldn't imagine what it would feel like to die this way, to be crushed to death. My ribs would break, my inner organs would—

"Help me, Leon!" I shouted. "How do I get out of here?"

Leon Worth is the smartest person I know. He's about four feet tall, and all of his limbs are pretty useless. He has a muscle disease called inclusion body myositis. It is slowly killing him. I wish somebody would find a cure for it. I've been helping him out for a few years. He's in a wheelchair, but he stands tall in my mind, as tall as anyone I've ever known. Shirley just adores him. Lots of girls do. And why not? He's a brave and amazing guy.

So as the walls kept grinding toward me, I thought of Leon. I called out to him again. "Help me!" He always has ideas; he can solve any problem. If I could just concentrate on some of the things we'd done together, some of the ways he'd dealt with difficulties, something would come to me. But time was running out.

"You know, you're a chick magnet," I remembered telling him just last week.

"James Bond on wheels," he responded. That had cracked me up.

Most people have a hard time understanding him. His voice is high-pitched and kind of wrecked, but I always know what he is saying. It bonds us.

He went with Shirley and me the second time we saw *Skyfall*. "I should be Q, you know," he told me afterward.

"Q!" I shouted now, petrified as the walls moved in on me. Q, the problem solver. I had to channel him. Think!

"And I should be Moneypenny and fall in love with you instead of Bond," Shirley had said to him. She was wearing the glistening gold earrings I'd got her for her seventeenth birthday, the ones that really make her dark eyes and short dark hair look great. She can really smile with her eyes. I love that about her. She was smiling at Leon.

"Chick magnet," I'd mouthed to him behind her back.

"Stud on wheels, a seated Daniel Craig," he said.

"What was that?" she asked. Anytime she heard the words *Daniel* and *Craig* together, she perked up.

"Stud muffin," he said, laughing.

"I'll say," she'd said and kissed him.

"Come on, Leon!" I yelled at the advancing walls. "Come on! How do I get out of here?"

He had come over to my place to stay that night. I'd let him sleep in my bed. I have to carry him out of the chair, even help him put on his pajamas and put him under the covers. I don't mind. It's the least I can do. Bad Adam isn't allowed in the room at those moments, not for one second.

"Hey," he'd said just before I turned out the lights to leave. "If I'm Q, then you have to be 007."

"I don't think so, buddy."

"No, no, you *are* Bond with all that Wing Chun stuff you know now, and you're a good-looking guy."

"Why, Leon, I didn't know you felt that way."

"Shut up, A-Murph. You *are* good-looking to girls, though I hate to admit it. Shirley knows."

"Well, Shirley is pretty bright, now that you mention it."

"So, if I'm Q, then I have to make you something."

"Like a gadget?"

"Yes, something you might even use sometime."

And so he had.

It was all coming back to me, and with it came a glimmer of hope in my desperate situation.

He'd come up with a plan for a pretty cool knife, built from the tiniest Swiss Army knife either of us had ever seen. We'd gone out together to buy it in Buffalo and then went to work on it, him instructing, me building. It didn't have just a blade, but also a little cell battery that could be used in all sorts of situations, even with the little flashlight we'd built into it. It also had a couple of tiny pellets the knife could actually shoot. Then we'd sewn it into the lining of a pair of my boots, right behind the steel arch support.

I had those boots on now! I hadn't even thought of the fact that I was wearing them when I went through airport security.

"This will be undetectable, hidden in the steel arch support," Leon had crowed after we'd put it into my boot. "It won't even get picked up on airport security."

I hadn't intended to test that theory and neither had Leon, I'm sure. But it *had* gotten through security.

And there it was now, in my boot, as the walls closed in on me.

But how could I use it? It was useless, wasn't it? *Think!*

I thought of Leon again. How inventive he was, how he never seemed to give up on anything, even though he was dying.

So I thought more about the boots. And that was when it came to me.

For our hidden little gadget, I'd bought these cool work boots that had steel toes. I liked the look of them more than anything else. They were black, with big soles that made me look even taller than my six-foot frame, and kind of had a Doc Martens vibe to them. The steel in each boot extended farther than usual, from the toe almost halfway down the shoe, and the clerk had bragged that it was as tough as titanium—in fact, it was some sort of special hard material a million times stronger than steel or something like that. I had big feet. I looked down at them.

The walls kept rumbling inward. They seemed to be picking up speed. They had reached the little desk and were beginning to crumple it! I looked up.

The ceiling was made of steel, just like the walls. I couldn't get out that way either.

I bent down, barely able to fit into the space now as I hunched over. My heart was pounding, and I was dripping with sweat. I ripped off the boots and tore Leon's knife out of the lining.

"Save me, little buddy," I whispered.

I snapped open the small blade and frantically started cutting up the shoes, ripping them in half just beyond the steel toes. The knife was sharp, but the leather was good and the rubber soles were thick. I sawed with everything I had. My hands were trembling. Soon I had to stand up to work. In a minute or two, I would be dead.

I fumbled the boots once I had them cut in half and dropped both of them. *Oh, God!* I could barely reach them now. I couldn't turn sideways anymore. There was only a few inches between me and the walls. It felt like my chest and back would be touching both walls if I took a deep breath. I wondered what it would feel like, and sound like, when my bones cracked.

My hands still shaking, I tore the steel toes out of the boots. They were each about four inches long, maybe a touch more. I lined them up so that they formed about an eight-inch length of extremely hard steel. I fitted them together so they wouldn't shift when the walls connected with them. Then I put them between the walls and prayed.

With my back against one wall, there was about an inch left between the other wall and my chest.

I screamed.

Less than an inch.

The walls groaned.

Half an inch.

A fraction of an inch from my body, the walls ground to a halt, held apart by the remarkable steel toes.

I felt like crying again.

I was safe, but for how long? How long would I be able to stand there? How long would the steel toes keep the walls from moving? Maybe this was worse than being crushed. Maybe I would just expire as I tried to stay on my feet. It would be a horrible death.

About a minute later, I could feel someone tapping on the outside of the building. Then I heard a voice. It was muffled. But it sounded like a girl.

SIX

AN ANGEL

I yelled as loudly as I could.

"IT'S ME! IT'S ADAM McLEAN! I'M IN HERE! YOU HAVE TO GET ME OUT!"

"Adam McLean?" I barely heard Angel say in that lovely accent. "My God, what's happened to the building? It's—it's—I'll go get someone!"

"NO!" I screamed. "NO! THEY ARE TRYING TO KILL ME!"

There was a long pause. Then I think she said, "I'll be back." There was silence. I prayed that was what she had said. Maybe it had been, "I'm not coming back." Maybe she was part of this whole thing; maybe she worked with Grandpa and was going to get him or his henchmen. She had seemed awfully unfriendly, awfully sour. I waited. Maybe Grandpa had ordered her to come out and save me. Maybe he was being forced to look like he hated me and wanted to kill me. Maybe it was the two henchmen who wanted me dead. Or maybe I had no idea what was going on. Only time would tell, a very short time. Would I die a horrible death or would this girl save me?

I was surprised at how together I seemed to be. I had had my moments of falling apart, but I was holding up well under the circumstances. When I'd heard her voice, I'd actually pulled myself together even more. Maybe it was a guy thing, an ancient-caveman, biological thing—I was trying to be a man, a hero…James Bond.

About five minutes later I heard a muffled sound above me. Angel had come back!

"There's a metal plate," she said through the wall, probably pressing her lips to it, "on top of the shed. It's about the same width as the whole building now. I'm going to try to unscrew it to see if I can open the roof."

"Thank you." It was a weird thing to say, almost British, polite and 007-cool in a tight spot. I don't know why I wasn't just screaming. Maybe I really was the sort of guy who was cool under pressure. I hadn't expected that, to be honest.

I tried to set aside the fact that at any second the steel toes could collapse and the walls would crush me. Angel might even see me die this gruesome way. I prayed she was handy with that screwdriver.

"Hurry, please!" I said as gently as possible.

I couldn't really hear very much, but with my hands on the walls I could feel the slight vibration from the pressure on the roof as she turned the screws. Then I could hear car horns in the distance, birds, the sound of the iron plate being pulled back. It was like hearing God speak to me.

"Hello," she said, looking down at me. Her face wasn't entirely clear in the darkness. Her shades were up in her hair, which, as usual, obscured her face. Funny, I thought, she must keep those sunglasses with her all the time.

"Hello," I said, trying to be cool.

She smiled at that, looking slightly impressed.

"Help pull me up," I said.

She must have brought out a stool or something and been standing on it in order to unscrew the metal plate. She paused for an instant and then reached down to take my hands. Her hands were small and warm. Bad Adam had some bad thoughts. I banished them and tried to help her pull me up. It was hard going. The space I was in was awfully narrow, but slowly, with her surprising strength and my agility, we were able to get my arms up above the roof of the building.

"It would be easier if your arms were smaller," she said, then blushed. Our faces were pretty close together at that moment. She projected a tough exterior, and that was the first time I'd seen her betray any sort of weakness.

I looped my arms over the top of the building and with one quick motion pulled myself right out onto the now tiny roof. As I did, my *Skyfall* T-shirt caught on something and ripped right from the top to the bottom, tearing it completely off. I leaped down from the building and looked at Angel, who was indeed standing on a stool. We were basically eye to eye, though she peered out through her messy hair. I had no shirt on, and her flashlight was trained in my direction. She glanced down at me and blushed again. Bad Adam was very pleased. I was in pretty good shape from all the weight training I'd been doing. But Good Adam was embarrassed.

"Sorry," I said and kind of covered up my chest a bit with my hands.

"That's okay," she replied, perhaps a little too quickly, and blushed a third time. Then she rolled her eyes. I could tell she was not too happy with herself. She struck me as the sort of girl who had maybe never had a date but was good at protecting herself, acting tough.

"I have to get a shirt."

"Yeah," she said. "Let's go into the house."

"But that's where they are."

"They?"

"Ssshh!"

She gave me a surprised look. "Okay, I'll go along with that...who do you mean by *they*?" She was talking in a near whisper now, as if we were in this together. She didn't ask why. She seemed to be enjoying herself.

"Jim and John and my grandfather."

"Your grandfather? Your grandfather is here? Is he visiting with you? I didn't notice him."

"He's that guy, Mr. Know."

"Oh." She gave me a puzzled look. "Really? He's never mentioned having a grandson, but then again, he doesn't talk much."

"He has seven of them."

"Seven?"

"In Canada and the United States. I'm the American, from Buffalo, New York."

"Uh, are you sure you have the right man?"

"It doesn't make sense to me either. Grandpa has lived in Canada since World War Two, although he flew planes for the US in the war. He died earlier this year."

I was so revved up that I didn't even realize how bizarre that sounded.

She took a step back. "Died?"

"But...but that's him, back there in the house. I mean, it's *him*, Mr. Know."

"You're crazier than he is." She kept her distance. "He isn't your grandfather."

"Yes, he is. And he and those butt-heads put me in that building and tried to kill me."

She looked at me carefully for a moment. "I know Mr. Know, as Jim and John call him, and he lives here in Bermuda in this house—he has forever."

"He's lived here forever? Really? Do you know that for sure?"

"Well, so I've been told. He's not my father or even my relative or anything. I—"

"How often do you see him?"

"Not too often, actually."

"*How* often?"

"Maybe once a week."

"So he could be flying in and out of here all the time."

"I suppose, but doesn't that seem a little un—"

"He's my grandfather and he tried to kill me. Either that or those two guys are controlling him."

"As nuts as that sounds, nothing would surprise me."

She was a strange one. Most girls would have been heading for the hills by now, after the stuff I'd just said. But here she was, still talking to me, saying kind of strange things herself. I'd never met anyone quite like her.

"Huh?" I said.

"I live a very weird life, to say the least. There are lots of things going on behind the scenes here. I figured out some of it. I'll tell you later. John and

Jim are not always very pleasant people. I'm sort of a prisoner here myself."

"A prisoner?"

"Well, not exactly. They don't hurt me or anything. They look after me and I go to school and—"

There was a noise from the house.

"Get down!" I said as loudly as I dared.

She didn't move. "Must be the dogs."

"Dogs?"

"He keeps a couple of pit bulls. I don't have much to do with them. Jim and John walk them every now and then, but I get the impression they stay in his room with him at night so no one can attack him. He's a really strange man—very eccentric, paranoid. He pays for everything for me and I have everything I want—at least, on the island. But he hardly ever even sees me."

I had wanted to sneak into the house and confront Grandpa. But pit bulls? Confronting him didn't seem like a smart thing to try at night. I needed another plan. For now, I just had to get out of here. But I needed my stuff. I couldn't go anywhere without my clothes, my passport, my airline pass and my Walther PPK, unloaded or not. Then I could get away and figure out what to do next.

"Where do they sleep?"

"He's in a bedroom deep in the house. I've never even been in it. Mine is right here, near the back wall. That's why I heard the Dahl building moving."

"Why do they call it the Dahl building?"

"Roald Dahl used to visit here. He even wrote in it. Those are his pencils and paper in there, or used to be."

"Roald Dahl? You're kidding, right? Why would he be here?"

"He was a spy too. Didn't you know that? He knew William Stephenson and Graham Greene and Ian Fleming, and he used to visit here."

"I've never heard of that first guy."

"The man called Intrepid? He was a Canadian, a very powerful man, maybe the greatest spy ever."

"First name William?" I said. I remembered the W shape on the gate at this house.

"Yes."

"Bill?" I remembered my taxi driver talking about the *man with a very common name.*

"I suppose so, yes. He used to live in Bermuda. I know he came here often. This house is full of spy things."

"Really? I need to know more about that. But first, will you help me get my things and get out of here? I have to get a hotel and regroup."

When she smiled, she looked like a girl who craved some adventure. She wasn't even asking me for more explanation. "Sure," she said and blushed again.

We sneaked back across the dark lawn and into the house, where Angel told me that Jim and John both had keys they kept attached to their belts under their suit coats. Those keys opened everything in the house. John was a light sleeper and, other than Mr. Know's, his bedroom was the deepest into the house; in fact, those two rooms were right next to each other. Jim, on the other hand, was in a more central room and slept like he was dead or something. Angel said she liked to get up and walk around at night, and John often appeared and asked what she was up to. She'd never ever seen Jim at night.

"Jim is our man," I said.

"Our man?"

"He's the one we have to steal the keys from."

"I'll show you the way," she said.

Moments later, we were inside Jim's bedroom. We obviously couldn't use the lights; we had to turn off Angel's flashlight and feel our way around. We got down on our hands and knees and crawled about on the floor until we found the bed. I motioned for Angel to go back to the door, and then I groped along the edge of the bed until I reached Jim. I knew the keys wouldn't be on his person. You couldn't sleep with keys on your belt. I reached under his pillow, the one his head was on. Bingo! There was a ring of about five keys nestled there. I was so excited that I pulled them out fast, and as I did, my elbow met a lamp on the night table and knocked it over. The room had a thick rug, so the lamp didn't make a sound when it hit the floor. But somehow, it connected with the switch.

The light came on.

Jim opened his eyes wide and looked at me. Then he leaped to his feet. I stepped back. I heard Angel inhale suddenly and whisper, "Oh god!" behind me.

Jim smiled. He looked like a middle linebacker in pajamas.

Believe it or not, I relaxed. That's what my Wing Chun master taught me: relax in a time of stress or combat. Use the element of surprise. This guy would have no idea that I could fight, and he certainly wouldn't expect me to fight *him*, of all people. He'd expect me to run or curl up into a ball or, at the very least, get defensive. I thought of the most lethal, aggressive move I knew, and I knew quite a few.

Attack before he expects it!

I spun on a dime and nailed him with a round-house kick, the flat part of the top of my right foot *splat* against his temple. He went down like a ton of bricks and lay still. Still breathing, but out cold. Perfect. I felt a little upset seeing him lying there, not moving at all. But Bad Adam was excited.

I turned and saw Angel right next to me. She had moved forward instinctively. She was so close that our faces were no more than a couple of feet apart.

"Wow," she whispered.

"Come on," I said. "Let's go to the office."

I turned off the light. She reached out and took my hand and led me through the dark house to the big office. When we got there, I rushed over to the desk and pulled open the top drawer, left side. Sure enough, my cell phone was there. And my bag was on the floor right next to the desk. But I stopped for a second. I could smell something, something familiar. A shirt was hanging over the chair right beside me. It must have belonged to Mr. Know. A light scent of after-shave or deodorant was coming from it. My heart sank. It was Grandpa's! There was no doubt about it. It smelled like him. I had been trying to convince myself that the man who had tried to have me killed wasn't really him, that he was a clone or something, or an identical twin, or an incredible three-dimensional virtual-reality image—*anything*. But this was *his* scent; this was how he'd smelled when he'd sat me on his knee and read *The Little Prince* and *The BFG* or *Fantastic Mr. Fox* to me when I was a child. Mr. Know *was* him, there was no doubt. Something deep and truly sinister was going on here. *You are a traitor*, someone had written. *You deserve to die.* The whole thing scared the living daylights out of me. Someone had known who and what he *really* was and had put it down in writing. Except Grandpa had hidden it. He's alive, I thought, and maybe *does* deserve to die. If only the other guys knew all this. They all thought he was dead! But I couldn't stand around thinking about it. I had to keep moving. I pulled another T-shirt out of my bag and slipped it on, pulled on a pair of ratty old sneakers I had brought and then stuffed everything else into the bag. I was good to go. But Angel stopped me.

"Let me look in there," she said, approaching the big desk. She pulled open the drawer and took something out. It was a passport: a Bermudian one. "I knew he had it in here somewhere. It's *my* passport. He keeps it from me."

We rushed out into the area near the front entrance, and I turned to say goodbye to her. I held out my hand. Bad Adam told me to kiss her right there, and then take her in my big, strong arms, tensing them so she could feel the muscles as I pulled her tightly to me. But I would never do something like that. Not anymore. Mostly because I would never betray Shirley, and I knew she would never betray me.

But Angel refused my extended hand.

"I'm coming with you," she said.

SEVEN

W

Angel had another surprise for me a few moments later.

We had gently closed the front door behind us, walked down the steep driveway, climbed over the fence and headed out onto the dimly lit residential streets of Paget Parish.

"You need to get out of here," she said, looking straight ahead. She wasn't very big, but she seemed to have lots of energy and strength. I had to step along to keep up with her. She sounded nervous.

"Yeah, as far away from the house as possible. Let's find a place to stay on the island. I have lots of money, enough for both of us. I'll pay for a room for you."

She looked at me funny, like she wondered why I had so much money. She was still wearing her gray sweats. She'd rushed into her room and come back in about thirty seconds with a small backpack. It looked to me like she'd need more clothes in a day or two. Only a guy could stretch whatever she had in her pack over more than a few days.

"No. I mean you need to get *right* out of here— off the island!"

"I can't do that. I came here to find out about my grandfather and I'm not leaving until I do. You don't understand. I *have* to know this!"

We were moving past pastel-colored houses, maintaining our fast pace, looking over our shoulders every few seconds.

"Adam, this is a small island. Not so small that everyone knows everyone or anything like that, but I can guarantee you that Jim and John and Mr. Know can find us fast, very fast. I've always thought they were capable of some pretty bad things, but I didn't know how bad…until I saw what they were trying to do to you. You can't mess with them. They'll be after us the second Jim comes around, which could be anytime now."

"But—"

"Look, I can tell you a lot about Mr. Know and what happens in that house. Maybe all you need to know."

"You can?"

"I've been watching and listening to what has been going on inside those walls for a long time."

I thought about my situation for a few seconds. "If we fly out of here, we're coming back, and coming back soon," I said. "I'll give it a day for things to calm down and then I'm returning. I have to." But I only had three or four days to solve everything. It was already the morning of December 28, about zero five hundred hours. Mom would be back from the Caribbean on the thirty-first. She and Dad were expecting me for a New Year's Eve party. Shirley would be there, probably looking great, hopefully having really missed me. I sure knew I missed her. I *had* to be there—not only there, but with all my questions about Grandpa answered. If I didn't make it, how would I explain things to Mom? Where would I tell her I'd gone? What would I tell her I'd been doing, and investigating? What would I tell her about her father? I had to know more, and I had to know it soon.

We were out on a busier road now. A few cars had passed by, and a cab was approaching.

"So," I said, "what can you tell me about—?"

"No time for that now. You have lots of money?"

"Yes."

"Enough for two plane tickets?"

"Two?"

"Yes." The cab was getting closer. She raised her hand to flag it down.

"I have a pilot's pass," I said, eyeing the cab. "I can fly anywhere I want."

"Really?" She smiled. "You are full of surprises, Adam McLean."

I still hadn't told her my real last name. Her accent was awfully nice. *She's mousy*, said Bad Adam. *Leave her behind.*

"I have more than enough money."

The cab stopped.

"Get into the taxi and don't say anything—not a word—until we're at the airport."

Once we were in the terminal, she made me get the tickets before she'd answer any questions. There was an early-morning flight to New York, just a few hours from boarding. She doubted Know and his people would look for us at the airport—at least, not at first. She seemed very excited about getting on this flight, almost too excited. She was trembling. What was I getting into, and why did she want to leave so badly?

"I am Guy Hicks's ward," she said once we'd sat down. We were in this little all-night café in the terminal. I had bought her a chai latte and I was having a Coke.

"Who is he?"

"Mr. Know."

"Okay, Angel, I'll play along. Why does he call—?"

She had a way of anticipating what you were thinking. It was a little scary. "I'm not sure. He's nuts, is all I know. He wants Jim and John to call him that, so they indulge him. It's like a game or something, a sort of spy game. I'm guessing he has so much money that they just do whatever he wants, for hefty salaries."

"But he's not Guy Hicks."

"He isn't?"

"He's my grandfather. Hicks is just an alias he's using."

"No, it isn't, Adam. He's *not* your grandfather."

"Yes, he is. Do you think I wouldn't recognize my own grandfather? And I have other proof, absolute proof."

"Okay. Enlighten me."

I looked around the terminal. No one was watching us. I was reluctant to tell her any of this. What if she was working for someone who was looking for the information I was about to give her? That seemed like a crazy thought. She was an eighteen-year-old girl (I'd caught her birth date on her passport when she'd flipped it open back at the house—I was getting good at snooping), and not an overly worldly one. She was so excited about getting on a plane, I wondered if she'd ever been on one before. She seemed harmless. But that's just what spies are like. They are not what anyone (other than actual spies) would expect. Le Carré had worked in the espionage world, and George Smiley, the character in his novels, was fat and short and old. He wore glasses and dressed in shabby clothes. He was both depressed and devious.

I looked at Angel, leaning forward with her chai latte pressed against her chin, warming herself like a little kid. What harm could it do to tell her? She had helped me escape and seemed to have some pretty serious issues with my grandfather and his thugs. She wasn't on their side. She was on mine—probably. I had no one else to confide in. She at least knew something about all of this. She was the only one who did, the only lead in what seemed like an awfully deep mystery. She was the only one who could provide a single clue.

"I'll tell you," I said. She smiled.

I told her about my grandfather, what a great guy he had been (which made me so sad that I almost choked up), about my mission for him in southern France, about him being a pilot and running some sort of mysterious import/export business for years, flying all over the world, gone for days and weeks at a time. I told her about all the stuff we'd stumbled upon at the cottage in Canada, including the envelope, the angry words on it and even the black Walther PPK.

"Wow," she said quietly. "Maybe Mr. Know *is* him."

It wasn't what I wanted to hear.

"Can I see the envelope?"

I hesitated for a moment, then reached down into my bag and handed it to her. She held it up to the light and examined it. As she did, I looked around, up and down the big hall of the terminal. At any second, Jim and John could show up. I wished the hands on the huge *WELCOME TO BERMUDA* clock above us would race forward. But that clock was like something out of Victorian England, and it seemed to move at about that pace.

"You missed something," she said.

"What do you mean?"

"See this?" She leaned toward me and held the envelope up to the light so we could both look at it. Her face and mine were just inches apart. She noticed and turned to look at me, right into my eyes through her hair. She swallowed. But I looked away and up at the envelope.

"Where?" I said.

"Right there, where my finger is."

I looked toward the tip of her right index finger. She hadn't manicured or painted her nails. They were just plain old fingernails. This girl wasn't what I was used to, that's for sure. I looked closely at the spot she was indicating on the envelope. Then I saw it. It was a letter.

W.

"What do you think that means?" I asked.

"I don't know, but it kind of scares me."

"Scares you? Why?" It had sort of scared me too. The gate at Mr. Know's house looked like a big *W*. William Stephenson—William with a *W*, an incredibly powerful man and big-time spy—apparently used to see my grandfather here. Why so many *W*s?

"Because, I, uh," said Angel, "I was just about to tell you something about that very letter."

"What?"

"Well, Mr. Hicks—"

"David McLean, my grandfather."

"Let's agree to call him Mr. Know."

"Okay, for now."

"He uses the letter *W* a lot, especially when he thinks no one is listening."

"Uses it?"

"I like to spy on him, so I know."

"You spy on him?"

"Well, you see, he adopted me. Like I said, I'm sort of his ward. I know that sounds awfully old-fashioned, like something from a Charles Dickens novel or something, but that's the word he uses. Technically, I'm Angel Hicks. He made up my first name. But he likes calling me Angel Dahl."

"Angel Dahl?" I said, thinking out loud. "That's good, very Bond. Ian Fleming would have loved that."

"Whatever." She didn't look too pleased. Then she paused and dropped her head as she spoke. "I was left on his doorstep when I was a baby. I was abandoned." She stopped again and sighed. "No one knows where I came from or who my parents were. Maybe they were from America or maybe the UK. At any rate, they didn't want me so they dropped me at the gates of a nice, secluded house in Bermuda, where no one would see them doing it. You know, wipe your hands of a problem in some faraway place and then disappear back to wherever you came from."

"I'm sorry."

"Yeah, sure, thanks. Whatever. It doesn't matter. But Mr. Know, nuts or not, has looked after me, or at least he's provided me with food and shelter and a good education. Not that I get along with anyone there. You wouldn't think someone like Guy Hicks would care about someone like me. And to be honest, I don't think he does. I think it just makes him feel like he's human or something, like he is at least doing something good with his useless, secretive life. Or maybe he just needs the company. I turned up at his door and he decided to not throw me out with the trash. Sometimes I wonder if he has an ulterior motive though. I used to hear him arguing about me with the guys who lived with him, still do— there's always been a Jim and John or a Peter and Paul, always two of them, always well armed, always looking out for Mr. Know. They usually laugh behind his back when they call him that, though they don't to strangers, like you."

"Tell me what he does. What are his habits?"

"He doesn't do anything, really. He's pretty secretive—keeps to himself and disappears a lot."

I nodded, not pleased to hear this. Like Grandpa, he was gone for days at a time. It seemed highly likely that David McLean had been living a double life. Part of it in Canada, part of it here.

"He seems pretty angry with the world. He argues a lot with John and Jim."

"Do you think he's a spy?"

The question didn't seem to surprise her. "I don't know, but he definitely has something to do with that kind of thing, somehow."

"How do you know?"

"Well, as I said before, I don't see him that often. He rarely even eats with me. My meals are prepared by a chef who comes by every day, and I eat with Jim or John. But I hear him talking about Ian Fleming and Roald Dahl and William Stephenson. He talks a lot about events in the sixties too, not to me but to John and Jim, and sometimes to himself or to the mirror when he doesn't think I hear him. Highly political things, like the Black Panthers, the Weathermen, the Bay of Pigs, JFK, Fidel Castro, the Cuban Missile Crisis. It's as if he knows something personally about those things. The Cuban thing is a big one with him. You must have studied it in school. You know, that time in 1962 when the Soviets and Nikita Khrushchev were discovered to have placed missiles in Cuba, aimed at the United States, and President Kennedy faced him down and almost brought the world to the brink of nuclear war between the superpowers. It would have destroyed the world as we know it. Mr. Know is pretty obsessed with that. But he talks about other spies too, not just Fleming, Stephenson or Dahl. He especially likes to talk about guys who defected, double agents like Donald Maclean and—"

"McLean?" My heart almost stopped.

"Oh yeah, I never thought of that," she said. She looked worried for a second. "Probably just a coincidence. Maclean wasn't the biggest double agent anyway, or the one that intrigues Know the most. He's more interested in Kim Philby."

"Never heard of him."

"He was a British operative who had been working for the Soviet Union, feeding them information. He defected there in 1963, the year after the missile crisis, actually, right about the time *Goldfinger* and *From Russia With Love* came out."

"Early James Bond movies," I said, almost to myself, "starring Sean Connery."

"Best Bond ever."

"That would be Daniel Craig."

"Good second choice and, I have to admit, awfully close. Fleming might have agreed with you. He wrote Bond to be more like Craig. He called him a 'blunt instrument.' That's DC."

"You seem to know a lot about spies," I said.

"I do."

"And about Bond, especially for a girl." (I think Bad Adam said that.)

"I do."

"Well, so do I."

"Probably not as much as me." I'd never heard a girl say something like that, and right to a guy's face.

"Oh, really?"

"Really. I've read every spy novel I can get my hands on, not just Fleming's. My favorites are the Le Carré and Greene novels. They tell the truth. Fleming was just making money. He wasn't much of a spy either, just an assistant in Naval Intelligence. A windbag, I'd call him, a bit of a poseur and not a nice man either: a real womanizer—that's where Bond gets that. William Stephenson, he was the real deal. And Fleming's books suck. If Bond really existed, he'd be dead within a week. Come on, a great-looking guy who uses a gun all the time and sleeps with a lot of women? He'd be easy to compromise. He'd be a liability. He'd stick out like a sore thumb."

"I agree. But Bond is great to watch."

"Well, Connery sure was, and Daniel Craig too. *Skyfall* was amazing."

"You'll admit that?" I teased. "You can stomach watching him, can you?"

She smiled. "Yeah, DC's all right." She paused. "Can I, uh, can I see the gun?"

I looked around and then slid my bag over to her. "You can't take it out. Just look." I unzipped the bag and snapped open the gun case.

She looked down and gave a little intake of breath. "Can I touch it?"

"I suppose. But don't take it out."

She reached down and held it in her hand, under cover of the carrying bag. "Never saw one of these before."

"Mr. Know doesn't have one?"

She laughed and sat back up. "No, I've never seen him with a gun. They don't seem to let him have one, which is curious. Or maybe he just doesn't need a weapon, given that they look out for him."

"Do you think someone is after him? Maybe that's why my grand—Mr. Know is so secretive, why he has to do what he does. Maybe he had no choice but to eliminate me. Or maybe he was planning to let me go?"

"Maybe." She didn't sound convinced.

"What about the W? You didn't finish telling me about that. You said he uses it a lot."

"Yeah, he really does. I've caught him doing it."

"Caught him?"

"I told you I like to spy on him. I've learned a lot about espionage techniques from reading. Because the house I grew up in seems to be connected to spying in some way, because Mr. Stephenson probably came there—and possibly Fleming too, and certainly Roald Dahl—I always wanted to know about it. I guess I thought it would help me learn more about who I am, perhaps where I'm from. Maybe I wasn't just left here; maybe there's more to it. So I haven't *only* read novels. I learned about the 'art of silent killing,' for example."

"What's that?"

"It's a way of fighting, taught by a guy named William Fairbairn long ago during the Second World War. It's manipulating people's spines, snapping bones, severing arteries, that sort of thing. Killing people without making a sound. They teach it to all the spies. I might even be able to do it, if push came to shove."

I tried not to laugh. Or at least I held Bad Adam back.

"And I've learned how to assume the color of the wall."

"Excuse me?"

"I can sneak up on people, be invisible. I can eavesdrop without people knowing. I follow Know sometimes. I listen to him when he talks to himself, which he loves to do."

"What does he say?"

"Well, he talks about W."

"How so?"

"He says stuff like, 'W knows.' And 'W marked the spot.' Sometimes he stares into his mirror and just says, 'W.'"

"What does it mean?"

"I don't know. It's all pretty weird."

"Is he referring to William Stephenson?"

"Maybe. But I don't think so. It's hard to guess what he's feeling when he talks about W. He seems to enjoy talking about Dahl or Greene or MI6 or the CIA, but when he refers to Stephenson he gets very angry. He never says why—he never explains anything, which is how you know he either once was or is a spy."

"Like Grandpa."

She ignored that and went on. "W, whatever it is, isn't a bad thing to Mr. Know. Or at least he's conflicted about it. He isn't *just* bitter about W...he both hates it *and* likes it...if that makes sense. But it means a lot to him. It sometimes seems like W is his whole life. It's like a secret of some sort."

It seemed to me that she was right. This letter obviously meant a lot to him. And it also seemed to me that if I could discover what *W* meant, I would uncover everything. I'd know why Grandpa did what he did, why he faked his own death and what he planned to do next.

An announcement came over the airport speakers. I jumped to my feet and looked up and down the terminal. I was terrified that Jim or John or Mr. Know—Grandpa himself, rolling forward in his wheelchair—were right there. But there was no sign of them.

The airport was simply announcing that boarding was about to begin for our flight to New York.

EIGHT

ADAM MCLEAN IN NEW YORK

Angel was awfully nervous during boarding and even more so once we were on the plane. When the engine powered up, she gripped my hand. Bad Adam enjoyed that in a different way than I did. I was glad to help her out. It felt good to actually be the one doing the comforting on an airplane. She dug her nails right into me when we took off. I tried to talk to her, but she shook her head. It wasn't as if she was totally frightened though. She seemed almost as excited as she was freaked out. She'd asked to sit in the window seat, and she pinned her head back against the headrest, eyes staring sideways out the window, as we went up. Once we had leveled off, she finally spoke.

"That's quite a sensation."

"You've never been on a plane, not once?"

"No." She almost seemed ashamed.

"But I thought you said Know has lots of money and looks after you."

"He does, but that doesn't extend to letting me leave the island."

"You've never been off Bermuda?"

"Only in my mind." She smiled and stared out the window again. "I can't wait to see New York!"

I had a sinking feeling that I'd been duped, that she'd used me to get off the island. Maybe that had been her job. Maybe I should still be back in Bermuda.

"You were right to leave the island, " she said, doing that mind-reading thing again. "If you want to get to the truth about all of this, we need to be somewhere they can't find us, at least for a while. That will give us a little time to talk about Mr. Know and about your grandfather. Maybe we can solve this. I can help you figure out what you need to know. Then you can either go home or come back to Bermuda and speak to your grandfather, and I'll go back, too, after I've seen New York. Jim or John will be coming after us anyway."

"They will?"

"Oh, yes. They'll be along shortly."

I thought of their gun holsters, their powerful builds, how angry they likely would be with me, the fact that my grandfather had ordered me dead, the Dahl building closing in on me, and I started to sweat.

"We really have to get away then, completely away. Maybe even out of New York. I can't go home. They've seen my passport, so they have my address." I was getting more and more frightened.

"I thought you wanted to figure this out, confront your grandfather."

"That too."

"Get away *and* confront them?"

We didn't talk for a while after that. She kept looking out the window, fidgeting more and more, her excitement obviously growing. I wondered again if all she really wanted was to get off the island. I started going back over what I had seen in Bermuda. Had I missed anything? Were there any clues in the things my grandfather had said? Was he trying to signal me that he was being held against his will? Had he sent this girl to save me? Was he just trying to scare me into leaving? It seemed awfully convenient that Angel just happened to be there to get me out of the Dahl building and then convince me to leave Bermuda— and fast. I glanced over at her. She was still gazing out the window, looking about twelve years old.

"What's up with the eye?" I asked her as a test.

She came out of her daze. "The eye?"

"The one on his desk—it's the only thing he keeps there. What does it mean?"

"I don't know. I've never heard him say a word about it."

If she knew anything, she wasn't saying. It was another dead end.

We had a W and we had a glass eye with a golden iris. And we had at least one deadly thug, maybe two, maybe two and their boss, in pursuit of us. Or so it seemed. The plane began its descent into New York.

I had been in New York a few times with Mom and Dad, and each time it had blown me away.

It's an amazing place. But for my companion, it was beyond that.

Angel Dahl was in heaven. She had her mouth open throughout the entire descent and kept it open through customs, the JFK terminal and even in the battered yellow New York cab we took to Manhattan. The much colder air didn't seem to bother her. She was wrapped up in a thick, long, double-breasted coat with a hood that I had bought for her at the airport. She didn't seem to want anything very trendy. She chose gray—her favorite color—and went for comfort rather than style. I still had my warm jacket in my bag.

I checked my texts as we zipped into the city. There was nothing from Shirley and a few from my cousins. I'd look at them later. But then I noticed that one was from Webb. I figured I should tend to that, help him out. He was on the trail of something mysterious, he said, but needed an Internet expert, a guy who could get him some obscure information and fast. I gave him Leon's number. Q could help him.

"That's where the Beatles played!" exclaimed Angel suddenly in my ear as the driver pointed out the Ed Sullivan Theater where David Letterman does his show. This girl is really stuck in the sixties, I thought. She wanted to see the Statue of Liberty and 30 Rock (they had satellite TV in Bermuda) and Yankee Stadium and Madison Square Garden— all of the Big Apple in a few bites. There were even some spy places she intended to check out, but 30 Rock—Rockefeller Center—was the place that most intrigued her. She said she'd always dreamed of going there, and not just because Stephenson had operated out of there during World War II. She said that it was actually a romantic place, with an outdoor skating rink and a gigantic Christmas tree at this time of year. People in love went there to skate. This talk about romance was surprising coming from her. *She's a chick*, said Bad Adam inside my head. *What do you expect?* Actually, I thought it was kind of sweet. But I was having none of any sightseeing. I wanted to get to a hotel, a big one where we could blend in. I had lots of money, so I could pick luxury accommodation, one with the added bonus of not being a place Know and his people would expect me to choose.

We went to the Hilton Midtown, where we booked two rooms, high up so Angel could have a view. I paid up front in cash, using assumed names, and added a bit for the clerk. That helped smooth everything out. (I had a credit card in my wallet that my parents had given me, only for absolute emergencies. I didn't want to use it now, since it could be traced.)

Mom and Dad had taken me to a few nice hotels, but this one beat them all. When you stood outside and looked up, the main part of the building looked like it went up to the sky, like many New York buildings. The lobby was circular, with gleaming marble floors and a statue in the middle. (Angel tripped over the rug at the front desk as she gawked at everything.) And the rooms were amazing, with incredible views, the type of lodgings only millionaires would feel at home in. It kind of made me feel good, pretty grown up and manly, to book rooms for Angel and me at a New York Hilton, *the* New York Hilton. She was smiling at me as we went up in the elevator. Me seventeen, her eighteen. I was the man. I had to keep Bad Adam from getting too excited.

I suggested to Angel that we stay in our rooms and see the city from our windows, at least at first. We shouldn't go out, I said, until we'd decided what to do next. I figured she'd go along with that, given the place we were in. But when we got together to talk, we got nowhere.

All through our room-service dinner in my room, we couldn't come up with a plan. Though, I must say, the meal was awfully good, and maybe it was throwing us off. I ordered a three-inch steak, smothered in mushrooms and onions, with fries, the coolest, sweetest, biggest, curliest fries of all time—I think Bad Adam gave that order—and she had a $40 hamburger with the works and another mountain of those killer fries. We topped it all off with cake for dessert. Hers was a triple deluxe deep-chocolate mousse—maybe there was a Bad Angel behind that order. I loved the fact that the bellhop referred to me as "sir" all the time, and she grinned when he called her "madam." I gave him a hefty tip.

But afterward, full as I could possibly be, I had no idea what to do. All we really knew was that Mr. Know seemed to be my grandfather, he talked about W all the time (*W knows, W marked the spot*), and he had a glass eye with a golden iris on his desk. I looked up the Cuban Missile Crisis on my phone. I learned a lot, but nothing that seemed to connect Bermuda or my grandfather to it—any such connection, to be honest, seemed kind of ridiculous. Angel told me everything she knew about Mr. Know, but that didn't seem to help either. Again I wondered how much she really cared, or if all she wanted was this trip to New York, this food, this hotel, this great time. When I finally wished her goodnight, I couldn't stop wondering: is she working for Grandpa?

I couldn't sleep. I kept tossing and turning, images of my grandfather's face in front of me, condemning me to death. He couldn't have really meant it. Perhaps John and Jim were supposed to just frighten me; maybe they were supposed to get me to go away or something, but they decided to really do it. Or maybe they were all working together, including Angel and the cab driver.

I was wide awake. I got up and went to the window and looked out. It was past midnight. New York, New York. The city that never sleeps. It was bustling down there, lights ablaze, people moving quickly along the sidewalks, yellow cabs still dominating the streets. The sky seemed lit up. America. My cousins hated it when I called it that. "It's the USA," they said, "the United States of America, NOT America. America is the whole continent, TWO friggin' continents! Including us and Mexico and all of..." I smiled. They were awfully sensitive sorts. But in a way, New York didn't really feel like part of America to me anyway; it was its own thing, very cool, very different. That's what got me about the 9/11 attacks. Why did they attack New York? NYC represents everyone, all of us, all different colors and kinds of people, all religions and cultures, the whole globe in one city. It's just a mind-blowing place. I wished I could go out with Angel and explore.

I like to sleep in my gotchies; they're not "tighty-whities" nor are they boxers. I favor the ones that are pretty snug and go halfway down my thighs. I was moving around the room in them now. I caught a glimpse of myself in the wardrobe mirror, full length. Bad Adam immediately thought I looked pretty good. Then he thought of the Walther PPK.

I walked over to the bag and took it out. Wow, what a piece of machinery! It kind of made me feel guilty to think that, but I couldn't help it. I could hear people in the hallway outside my room. It sounded like girls, young women, two of them. Here I was in my underwear, a gun in hand, with two young women right outside my door. Bad Adam thought that was pretty cool. He convinced me to strike a James Bond pose. I gripped the gun in my right hand, leaped onto the bed and pointed it straight at the mirror, crouched and ready for action, just like Daniel Craig and all the other Bonds, including Connery, in the opening sequences to the movies, music swelling. I could hear it now, a big orchestral sound, with lots of horns. At that very moment my door opened! Someone had jimmied it and entered!

I suppose I should have swung around and pointed the gun at the intruder. But I was so shocked that I only turned my head. I knew it was John or Jim. Either one would be able to take me out instantly.

But it was neither of them, most definitely not. It was the two young women.

Angel mustn't have pulled the door all the way closed when she left.

"Oh!" said one of the women. "Oh my!" She looked about twenty, dressed to kill, wearing tight black leather pants, a nearly see-through white blouse and lots of makeup. She was blond and shapely and had some sort of accent—Swedish, maybe. I could smell her perfume instantly. Her scent was amazing.

"Oh my, yah," said the other one, who wore a short red skirt that accentuated her long legs. Her shining auburn hair looked like she'd put sparkles in it. She had an accent too. German, I thought at first, or Russian. She pulled the door back and glanced at the number on the outside. "We thought this was *our* room!"

"So sorry," giggled the blond. "We're across the way."

"Yes, sorry…sir."

But they didn't move. Remember, I can pass for twenty-one sometimes. They kept staring at me. It sounded like they were both a little tipsy.

"You, uh…look good," said the blond in her deadly Swedish accent, smiling very wide and showing perfect white teeth that contrasted with her bright red lipstick.

"Ya, you do," said the other, and they both burst out laughing and then left the room. I could hear them in the hallway, whispering. Then they were quiet.

After them, said Bad Adam. *This is your James Bond moment! TWO Bond girls!*

But I slumped down on the bed. I didn't even make a move to get up and properly shut the door, which was still slightly open. What an idiot, I thought. I sat there for about a minute, looking out the window from the bed, feeling like a fool, wondering about my grandfather again.

Then there was another noise at the door.

This would be John or Jim! Maybe both!

I turned and trained the gun at my intruders, a nearly buck-naked James Bond ready to act. I didn't have a single bullet, but they wouldn't know that.

"Oh!" said the face that was peeking around the door. It looked a little shocked but equally intrigued.

It was the Swedish girl again. She'd let her hair down. It was glowing as if she'd brushed it about a million times. "Are you going to shoot me?" she asked. She didn't sound afraid. She sounded interested. She stepped inside this time. "My name is Britt and this—" she turned to the door and it opened farther "—is Ursula." The German girl made her entrance.

Bingo! said Bad Adam.

"May we come in?" asked Britt.

"Yes—no!"

"Yes?" asked Britt.

"No?" said Ursula and offered a sort of pout, her substantial lips, painted with even glossier red lipstick now, pursing together and her eyes growing wide and innocent-looking.

I opened the wardrobe and pulled out the hotel housecoat and quickly put it on. I had made up my mind. But then I looked at them again. They were both gorgeous and very interested…in me.

"I have a girlfriend," I said quickly, before anything else could come out. "You have to go."

If Bad Adam could have punched me, he would have.

"What?" asked Ursula. She seemed a little shocked.

"No fun tonight?" said Britt in that Swedish accent.

"You have to leave. This isn't your room. Go home."

"James Bond wouldn't say that," said Britt, looking at the gun, which I'd thrown on the bed. It was her turn to pout, looking up at me with puppy-dog eyes.

"Well, I'm not him," I said. "Guns are bad things." I don't know why I said that last bit. It didn't make much sense (or maybe it did). But I said it, just blurted it out. They left, with real pouts on their faces.

Seconds after they went out the door, Angel came in.

"I heard some noise." She glanced back at the women, fumbling with the key to their own room across the hall; they weren't pleased. "Who are they?"

"Two ugly drunks."

"They didn't look ugly to me."

"You must have left the door open. They came in by mistake. I asked them to leave."

"You did?" She looked pretty surprised. Then she smiled.

"I have a girlfriend, Angel. I should have told you that too. You should go. We need some sleep. I'll see you in the morning. And my name is not McLean. It's just Adam Murphy."

Her smile faded. She looked like she didn't know what to do or say now, to admire me or be a little ticked off. But out the door she went.

"You're a good guy," she said over her shoulder as she left.

I looked into the mirror. *You're an idiot*, said Bad Adam, right to my face.

I tried to sleep again. But it was hard. I forgot about the girls in seconds, but my grandfather kept coming to mind again and again. I got up and walked around the room. Then I went to the door and looked through the little spyhole. I like doing that in hotels. It seems so strange and quiet in the hallways at night, and you have a kind of a skewed, fish-eye view. Everything was quiet out there. But then I saw something. Angel. She had changed her clothes and was sneaking out of her room in perfect silence, rushing off down the hall toward the elevator with something under her arm.

NINE

PURSUED

I had my clothes on in a flash and was soon following her. But she had vanished. I whipped along the corridor, pulling my jacket over my T-shirt and getting anxious. I looked up at the panel above the elevator doors and saw numbers lighting up in descending order, heading all the way down to the lobby. I realized now what she had been carrying—her coat. Angel was going out! She was *sneaking* out!

I took the stairs and must have done five steps at a time, fourteen flights down. With my long legs, it took me about five seconds per flight. It seemed like no time before I was in the lobby. I looked out over that huge circular room with the marble floor and spied her all the way across it, about to go through the revolving doors into the street. She glanced behind her as she did, and I darted behind a pillar.

I had no idea how to tail someone. I'd only seen it in the movies. But I had to follow her. I had to know what she was up to. This might be the key that unlocked everything.

She didn't make things easy for me. She moved as if she knew someone actually *was* tailing her. That made me even more suspicious. She strode quickly and nimbly, in and out of the surprisingly thick crowds that were funneling down the wide Avenue of Americas from our hotel's location near Fifty-Fourth Street. She glanced back occasionally, but most of the time she simply moved quickly, looking straight ahead, sometimes craning her neck up at the amazingly tall buildings that lined every street in midtown Manhattan. During the day, the crowds had been so dense—absolutely packing the sidewalks—it was evident to us that it would be hard to get places fast, though many New Yorkers seemed to know how to negotiate their way around that problem. They were expert crowd wranglers. It helped that no one seemed to pay any attention to the streetlights. People just moved. If you stopped in New York, it seemed you might not get going again for a while. Every block had great stores and famous buildings. The loud sounds of cars and horns and voices and the gas fumes from all the vehicles, mingled with the smell of the big New York pretzels and chestnuts roasting at the food trucks, made for an awesome scene. Even at this hour, there was a buzz. It was indeed the city that never slept.

I had to keep Angel within view and not pay any attention to the sights. Earlier, I had made sure she had money, and the only time she slowed now was to give some to beggars. She seemed to stop at every one she passed, and there were quite a few. I began to wonder if this nice person, as she was beginning to appear to be, could really be fooling me, working against me somehow. Despite her strange and unloving upbringing, and her occasional sourness, she seemed to have an innate kindness. She cared about others. She seemed to care about me. Was she helping me somehow? But where was she going?

We passed huge glass buildings and others made of concrete. Then we passed Radio City Music Hall, and she kept walking, all the way down to Forty-Seventh Street. There she turned right, and about a block farther, we were at Broadway, perhaps the most famous street in the world. Though New York is always lit up, 24/7, Broadway seemed even brighter. Then I realized why. We were approaching Times Square.

Some people, mostly Americans I guess, call it "The Crossroads of the World." And it is amazing: a legendary city square in the shape of a bow tie that stretches several blocks south from 47th along Broadway. It's where they always do the New Year's Eve celebrations, where all the American morning TV shows like *Good Morning America* and *The Today Show* are broadcast. It's right near famous theaters too. And it seems as though every popular clothing store in the world is here, from Aeropostale to Forever 21 and The Gap. But perhaps what stands out most are the billboards. They are massive! And many are really just humongous digital screens, football fields of light, advertising jeans or cell phones or whatever you need or don't need. It's kind of America at its best. Or worst—I'm not sure which. In a way, it's kind of like my Walther PPK: it's awfully exciting, but it doesn't seem like it's entirely good either. "Sodom and Gomorrah," I've heard it described as—I'm not exactly sure what that means, but I don't think it means heaven.

As Angel crossed into the square, I could see her slow down, almost stagger, and look up. Times Square must have seemed absolutely incredible to her. Here in the early hours of the morning, the place was packed, and it was lit so dramatically it seemed like the middle of the day. She was staring up at a billboard for Guess Jeans that made the model look like she was a thousand feet tall, a sort of giantess, a goddess of our times—her open mouth, painted with scarlet lipstick, seemed the size of my entire body.

There's actually a grandstand right in the street in Times Square, a set of red bleachers where people, tourists mostly, can sit and watch the commotion— watch life move past at jet speed. Angel fumbled her way up onto one of the benches. I say "fumble" because she seemed to be unable to take her eyes off the scene before her and was feeling around with her feet as she stared in the opposite direction. I couldn't go up there or she'd see me. I had to stay on the street and watch, but I wanted to do that from the front, so I could observe her face. I crossed behind the bleachers and walked over to the other side of the square and leaned against a building where it would be hard for her to spot me. I was beginning to feel relieved. It seemed like she didn't have any devious motives: she simply wanted to see New York at night. And who could blame her? I watched her for a few minutes. Her face glowed as she gazed at the scene. She looked innocent and sweet. My heart went out to her. Then I stopped myself. I needed to think of Shirley. *Angel is mousy anyway*, said Bad Adam. But it was hard not to admire this kind, intelligent girl.

Then I saw something that changed everything. Walking down Broadway, on the far side of the bleachers, still wearing just a suit despite the cold air, muscles bulging through his clothes, gun holster evident, breath coming out in clouds from his mouth, was a blond man I instantly recognized. *John!* He was wearing his spy shades. In the midst of this cornucopia of the world's citizens, he stood out.

My heart began to thump. I didn't know what to do. For a moment, I simply froze. Was Angel in danger? Would John exact revenge against her for helping me? Did he have orders from Grandpa?

John seemed to be examining everything and everyone as he walked. He talked to a few people and was checking out the crowd, always keeping an eye on the bleachers. Then he began moving toward it.

Angel suddenly stood up. Could she have spotted him in the crowd? He was getting awfully close. She began quickly descending the bleachers, going directly toward him!

It suddenly occurred to me what was *really* going on. *They were here to meet!* This must have been prearranged! I had been wrong about her.

Both terrified and intrigued, I felt for the Walther PPK, which I'd tucked into my jacket. It was a stupid thing to do. I didn't even have any bullets. But I hadn't wanted to leave the gun in the hotel.

Should I watch or should I intercede? A funny thought ran through my mind. What would James Bond do? That must have been Bad Adam thinking, plotting with his stupid TV/movie/bad-side-of-America imagination instead of with his brains.

There was no doubt that John had spotted Angel. And she definitely knew it was him. Her face had become tense. Another thought shot through my mind. Did she know I had followed her?

Had she brought me to him? Were they setting me up? I remembered that wherever James Bond was, he always made sure he had an avenue of escape. I looked around. What was the best way out of here? What would a real spy do? I couldn't remember what George Smiley had said about this in the Le Carré novels, if he'd said anything at all. He'd likely just slip away, disappear into the crowd.

But what if I was wrong about what was going on here? Was Angel in danger?

In seconds I had the answer. It was an emphatic yes.

She was trying to get down the bleachers as fast as she could. I stepped away from the wall and moved through the crowd toward her, ready to either sprint to her rescue or run away from her. I could see that she was shaking, and as she reached the bottom of the first tier of bleachers, she turned away from the beeline John was making toward her. He was trying to look inconspicuous, calm on the surface, but his hand had moved toward the holster on his chest and he had fixed his gaze on her. Or so it seemed, since his eyes were hidden behind those jet-black shades.

I made for Angel.

She spotted me and her face brightened a little. We were now moving toward each other. I thought I could get to her before he did. I actually ran in her direction, negotiating my way through the crowd, pushing people out of the way. It was New York, so no one seemed to notice. I got to her just as she jumped down from the last step and John was within a few yards. I pulled her toward me. She almost collapsed into my arms, which was the only thing that made me feel good at that moment. We pivoted together and moved as fast as we could across the Square, using the crowd to keep him away from us. She gripped my hand. Her hand was warm, even in the cold New York night. I could feel her shaking. We bobbed and weaved through the herds of people, stepping in front of some pedestrians, behind others, putting some distance between us and our pursuer. But I doubted that would last for long.

The crowd was still thick at the bottom of the square near the famous One Times Square building, the place where the ball drops on New Year's Eve. It also had the news of the day rushing along on an LED crawl about a story or so up. It said something about terrorists found on American soil, about the guns they'd been able to get. But we had no time to watch it. We dodged through the crowd and got out onto famous Forty-Second Street. There weren't as many people here, which was both good and bad. It was harder to hide, but we could move much faster. If we could motor though, so could John.

"We should find a policeman and tell him that we're being chased!" I yelled.

"What would we say?" she cried. Would we say that I thought my grandfather was a vicious man, a suspected double agent and spy who had tried to kill me? Did I want to do that? And wouldn't John just disappear if we approached a cop? And then it would be us who would have to explain why we were complaining to the police about being chased by no one. I doubted they would take kindly to that at all.

As the crowd thinned even more, our pace picked up. Then we started to jog, and then we ran. I play a little football, some hockey and even do track and field. I used to care pretty intensely about winning all the time. Not anymore. The most important thing is to be a good teammate, though Bad Adam often tries to tell me I shouldn't pass so much in hockey.

Anyway, I can really move when I need to, which is why it shocked me that Angel could almost keep up with me. She was a surprising girl. And I had the feeling that there were more surprises to come.

She shook my hand loose, almost as if to say that she could run on her own, thank you very much, but also to allow me to get away.

I wanted to keep her with me. I glanced back, puffing and sweating. John had emerged out of the crowd on the south side of 42nd and locked onto us. He started to run. I imagined that he could move even better than us. He was big and powerful, but without an ounce of fat on him.

And so we all sprinted. No one in the street seemed to notice. And we couldn't cry out for help. Or could we? Maybe we could fake that he was a thief or someone trying to assault us. But we both seemed to know, instinctively, that John could take any idea like that and turn it around. The best move was to simply get away from him.

But he was gaining on us.

I reached back, pulled Angel toward me, stepped in front of a big group of people in African headgear and long gowns, and turned west onto

Thirty-Ninth Street. We lost John, but only for a few seconds. We kept running, turning left on Seventh Avenue and going south. We happened to hit the light perfectly, and this time the pedestrians had to stop, since the traffic was moving. But when I looked over my shoulder, anxious and breathing hard, I could see John taking a shortcut, knifing his way across Thirty-Ninth Street right through the traffic. For a second, I thought he was going to meet his death. But he seemed expert at getting through the lines of reckless big-city vehicles. How does a Bermudian do that? Or was he actually from somewhere else?

On we went across the tight New York blocks, ignoring lights, crossing busy streets, putting ourselves in danger, across Thirty-Eighth, Thirty-Seventh, Thirty-Sixth, all the way down to Thirty-Forth until we could see Madison Square Garden—"The Most Famous Arena in the World," as it's known in America. I could picture my cousins rolling their eyes at that too.

It was attached to the Pennsylvania Railway terminal, or Penn Station. It was kind of behind and above the station, a big round building like a massive gray cake. I could see two giant banners outside, each the height of a three- or four-story building, one an image of a New York Ranger, the other of a New York Knick. But at this hour, it wasn't particularly crowded; there weren't lineups teeming outside. I wondered if we could go through the train-station entrance, down the stairs or escalators in a flash and mix with people inside—there would likely be a warren of tunnels in there where we could twist and turn and try to get away.

But as we finished crossing Thirty-Third Street, John was reaching the other side. He was that close. Two policemen dressed in the distinctive blue of New York cops, looking tough like they all do, stood in front of the train station's entrance. I wished we could just seek their help. We were about to be caught! I had no idea what John would do. I tried to become calm, readying myself for a little Wing Chun. But John likely knew what I had done to Jim back in Bermuda. I wouldn't have the element of surprise this time. I didn't like my chances.

Then Angel betrayed me.

TEN

MOVIE MOMENT

I was just a few strides in front of her.

"Adam!" she cried out. I thought John had her, but when I turned, he was still about twenty feet behind. Was she giving up? I had to go back and protect her. I slowed down and stepped toward her. She ran right into me, wrapped her arms around me for a while, lingered there in the midst of all this and then let go and booted past. What was she doing?

"Officer!" she shouted. She was running toward the cops.

"Angel! Don't!" Had she lost her mind? Was she so desperate that she was giving everything up to the police? John would just get away! *We* would be the ones in trouble.

"This man is chasing me!" she cried. "He groped me! Up on Thirty-Fourth Street!"

For an instant I wondered why in the world she would put it that way. Why would she characterize John's actions like that? If she felt she had to do this, if she had to finger him, even though he would simply vanish the second he heard her cry out, why did she say it like that? *Groped her?* Why didn't she say he had a gun and was after both of us?

Then I realized why she was saying it. And I realized who the *he* was in her accusation. She was pointing at the man she was accusing of assaulting her. But it wasn't John. It was me!

"What?" I cried. "It was him!" I turned around to point out our pursuer. But he was gone. He had disappeared, just as I had suspected he would. There was no trace of him on Thirty-Third Street, Seventh Avenue or anywhere else. People were walking past, going about their business, unaware of or uninterested in our little drama. But I had the feeling he was watching from somewhere. I just couldn't see him. He had assumed the color of the wall or, in this case, the New York crowd.

"Angel, how could you do this?"

One of the cops stepped toward me and took out his gun. The other guy pulled Angel behind him and reached for his weapon too.

"Just relax, sir, and get your hands out where I can see them."

I did as he said. He approached quickly, holstering his gun as the other guy trained his on me. Not a single pedestrian even looked our way!

Then I realized something else, something bad, something really bad. He was going to frisk me. My heart sank. The Walther PPK! Not only was I not going to find out about my grandfather, I was also going to go to jail for possession of a firearm.

But what happened next shocked me even more. The cop got me to lean against a wall, frisked me up and down and said, "He's clean." And he was right. The PPK was gone! Either I had dropped it or someone had—

I looked over at Angel. I couldn't tell whether she was trying to hide a smile. Her expression seemed awfully straight, kind of poker-faced. But I knew she had the gun. She had snatched it when she purposely ran into me. Why had she done that? She most definitely had the deft hands of a spy. She had my gun for good too. They wouldn't frisk her—she was the victim. Is that what she wanted? Was it all about the PPK? Then I thought of something. Walther—it began with a *W*. The gun! Was the gun W? Was there something in it? A map? A message? Was that why she took it?

But it didn't matter now. If I told them she had a gun, they'd likely just laugh and I'd never see it again. I was willing to bet that Angel had never even told me her real name. I knew it wasn't really Dahl, but maybe it wasn't Hicks either.

"Let's get you into a car, sir," said the cop. My heart was absolutely pounding. I was being arrested for assaulting a woman in New York City! I couldn't believe it. Not even Bad Adam would do something like that. What would my parents say? What would I tell them when I exercised my rights and made my one call? Or do they even let you do that? Is that just a TV thing? Would I be put in a New York jail cell with hardened criminals? I was trying very hard not to cry. And I had thought Angel was a kind person. Who was she and what did she want? Would she meet up with John once I'd been taken away? Why did she save me in Bermuda just to do this to me here? Now I'd never know about Grandpa, about that eyeball on his desk, about W. Or was Grandpa behind what had just happened too?

The cop cuffed me. The cuffs cut into my wrists. I glanced back over my shoulder at Angel, now standing by the Madison Square Garden entrance. She was talking to the other cop, likely giving him as much incriminating evidence as she could, to really put me away. She wouldn't even look at me. I kept trying to fight back the tears. James Bond wouldn't cry. But this was real life.

"Watch your head," said the cop as he opened the back door, pushed down on my head and gently eased me into the car. It was tight in the backseat. It was separated from the front by a steel cage. I imagined who else had been cuffed and put in this squad car. Murderers? Rapists? Gang members? The tears were coming to my eyes. But I was determined to be tough. Relax, I told myself. Think this through. Find a way to get out of it. But there didn't seem to be any way out. Angel had me. I never could have dreamed that this girl, so innocent on the outside, would have been the one who wrecked my life. *She's mousy*, Bad Adam had said. I agreed!

But less than five minutes later, the cop received a phone call and everything changed again. He listened for a few minutes, then said, "Okay." He glanced back at me. "We're letting you go." He was kind of shouting. Everything this guy said was loud, even the good things. He didn't know how to be subtle.

"You are?"

I couldn't believe it. I felt like shouting myself, even louder than him. But I tried to stay composed.

"You're lucky. She ain't pressing charges."

"She isn't?"

"No, she says she might have been mistaken. I'm guessing she knows you and you were getting rough with her and she loves you, you chump. Take my advice and clear out—stay away from her. And don't touch a woman that way again. Don't even think about it. You got me?"

"Yes, sir." I moved sideways to get out of the car.

"Stay put."

"Huh?"

"I'm taking you about twenty blocks south. Far away from her, in other words." He didn't say "words," though; he said "woids." Great New York accent, which I'd barely noticed in my fear.

"And don't try to find her. My partner's taking her somewhere else too."

We drove south. He broke every traffic law they had and ignored every light. He also started to chat.

"Knicks fan?"

I could be a woman beater and he was asking me about basketball?

"No, hockey."

"Rangers?"

"No, Sabres."

"Who are they?" he said, and he didn't seem to be joking. "Tried the New York hamburgers? Check out a place on Thirty-Second and Fourth, name of Julio's; talk to Big Julio. Heart attack burgers, we call them. They're the best."

Ah, New York.

Ten minutes later, he let me out in Greenwich Village, which is this cool, artsy area that seems almost like a little town inside the city and is full of very hip restaurants. Beatniks used to live here in the fifties, hippies in the sixties. I'd read that in social studies class.

I rubbed my sore wrists when I got out. I was alone in New York. What would I do now? It seemed to me that my best bet was to get on the subway and head straight back to the hotel. My clothes were still there. Luckily, I'd grabbed my wallet and passport and my hoard of money before I'd gone out the door. I hadn't wanted to leave them behind in a hotel room, locked or not. The cop had checked all my ID in the cruiser and handed everything back before he let me out.

Then something hit me. It hit me hard. He hadn't said anything about the huge amount of money that was in my wallet. In all the excitement, I hadn't realized how light it felt. I pulled it out of my pocket and opened it. It was empty! I'd had a stash of about five thousand American dollars in there, what remained of what I'd taken out of the hole in the wall in the cottage. It had been in hundred-dollar bills. There was nothing left! *The cop had stolen it!* I stood stockstill on the street, my mouth wide-open, my stomach churning. "He couldn't have," I said out loud.

And I was right. He *couldn't* have. He *wouldn't* have. Even New York cops aren't that corrupt. There was something odd about all the frisking he'd done though. There was a trend to it. He didn't find the pistol because Angel had it, and he didn't find the money because... *it hadn't been in my wallet when he looked!*

I was at about Eleventh Street. I started running up Seventh Avenue toward midtown. I wasn't sure why. How would I ever find Angel? Angel and the PPK and the five thousand she had stolen! I had given her lots of money in case she needed it. But she'd wanted all of it! I had thought I could trust her. Then I recalled Le Carré: spies weren't to be trusted.

"What's the deal with Angel Dahl?" I said out loud as I rushed uptown. Was everything about her fake? No, she was just a thief; that's *all* she was. An abandoned child with a messed-up childhood and a grudge against everyone. She was using my money—Grandpa's money—to do whatever she wanted in New York City. I'd never find her here! Or was she booting it back to Bermuda, back to a house I wouldn't be able to get into again without being caught and killed?

But then I started *really* thinking about her. Would she *really* do this? I thought of her walking in front of me a few hours ago, when she didn't know I was behind her, giving money to every street person she met. I thought of her quietly saying to me, "You are a good guy," in that beautiful, soft Bermudian accent. I thought of her helping me out of the Dahl building.

I thought of the way she had started looking at me, how she blushed when she saw me with my shirt off. And I also thought something else.

What a brilliant move it would have been if she had planned all of this! It would have been a stroke of genius. Here she was, being pursued by a man that she and her friend (a boy) could not get away from, so because she was the girl, she found a cop, causing the pursuer to make himself scarce. She pretended the boy had just assaulted her, then said she wouldn't press charges and asked the cops to take her somewhere else in the city, far away from the pursuer, knowing that the cops would also take her boyfriend (uh, her friend, that is) far away too. And just before all this happened, just an instant before, she bumped into her friend, whom she knew the cops would frisk, lingered there with her arms around him and in his coat and relieved him of his gun and even his suspicious clip of a massive amount of money, and took it with her for safekeeping. Then she met up with her friend somewhere else, both of them free of their pursuer and ready to move on…together. It would indeed be genius, a perfect way to escape an inescapable situation.

But wasn't that a fantasy, a movie plot? Would she actually do that, this outwardly unremarkable young woman with the Bond Girl name? And if she did do it, where would she go afterward to meet this boy? Where in this massive, crowd-filled city would she go? It would have to be somewhere that I knew about, some place she had mentioned to me. I thought of her in the cab coming into New York, her blue eyes staring up at the buildings in awe. I thought of her talking about the city as if it were the place of her dreams. Then it came to me. She'd said something about a particular place she wanted to see the most.

30 Rock!

I started to really run. I didn't care about the subway anymore, I was booking it north on my own two feet at a million miles an hour, heading for Forty-Ninth Street near the Avenue of Americas and the Rockefeller Center.

On the way, I kept telling myself not to get my hopes up. Why would this girl care about me and my need to know the truth about my grandfather? It was my life, my world, and it couldn't possibly matter to her. She'd been abandoned at birth; she was likely hardened inside. My view of her as kind, despite what had been done to her, seemed awfully naïve. She wouldn't be there.

It took me about twenty minutes to get up to Forty-Ninth Street. I'm guessing it would take most people about an hour and a half. I was sweating bullets. It was hard not to stare up at 30 Rock when I turned the corner to the side of the building where the skating rink was—it was so famous. And there was the rink. That was what she said she dreamed of—not the TV show. She dreamed of the ice rink where people in love came to skate.

But she wouldn't be there. It was a long shot beyond long shots.

The rink wasn't visible from the sidewalk or even from the plaza beside the building. It had been built below the surface, about twenty feet or so below ground level. Even though it was about three in the morning, I could see people standing around the gray concrete walls, looking down at the skaters. There were American flags above us, of course, lining the concourse—you've got to wave the old red, white and blue. But there were flags of other countries too. *Good for you, New York.* I spotted the Canadian one and smiled.

But I couldn't spot Angel. She wasn't up here anywhere. I felt like collapsing. I could barely hold myself upright against the wall. I had lost all the money, the gun, the chance to redeem my grandfather. All I had now was the fact that he had tried to kill me. What would I tell my cousins? What would I say to DJ? I looked up at the top of the giant Christmas tree and the star that meant hope to so many people. I gazed down along the big green branches, all the way to the skaters. Then I saw something I could barely believe. Down there, looking out at them, leaning over a gate near the bottom of the tree so she would be easy to find, looking as if she wanted to be out there on the ice, skating with someone special, her face red from the cold, was Angel Dahl.

I just stared at her. I almost felt like crying again. But this was a different sort of emotion. And it wasn't only because my money was safe. It was something deeper. And it took me by surprise. I was over-joyed to see her, to see Angel. *She's mousy*, said Bad Adam. "No, she's not," I said out loud. "She's a good person—a great person." When I said that, I thought of Shirley. She's even better, I told myself quickly. I can't wait to see her again. But the feeling I put into

131

it faded a bit when Angel turned her face directly to me, some fifty yards away, and found me in the crowd, first glance. Then she opened up her big gray coat—sort of secretively, like a spy—and barely revealed something inside. Even from where I stood, I could see that it was the Walther PPK, tucked into the waistband of her pants. She patted a pocket with the other hand, where the stack of money must be. I smiled at her. She smiled back and motioned for me to come to her.

ELEVEN

THE MEANING OF THE EYE

She looked like she wanted a hug, but I shook her hand and gave her a pat on the back instead.

"Good thinking, excellent thinking," I said. She gave me a weak smile.

Up close to Angel, I realized how silly I was being about her. Sure, she was a nice girl, but I had actually been imagining that I was starting to like her. She wasn't Shirley, who had stood by me through all the times I hadn't been so nice. My girl was one in a million. She was at home, looking out for Leon, waiting for me. I told Angel we needed to take a deep breath and think about what we had to do next.

I pulled out my phone and texted Shirley, telling her I was in New York, checking out something about Grandpa.

I know that sounds weird. It's a bit complicated. I'll fill you in later.

I expected her to text right back. But she didn't. Of course, I thought, she's asleep.

"Let's go back to the hotel," I said. "We can talk on the way."

"I don't think that's such a good idea."

"Why? John doesn't know where we're staying."

"I wouldn't count on that."

"Really? How would he know? I used assumed names."

"If he's got anything to do with the CIA or MI6, he'll know. They can find anyone, anywhere."

"CIA? Surely you don't think he's—"

"I don't know what he is—that's my point. I don't think we should take any chances."

She was right. But all our clothes were back there. And we both had to get some shut-eye. Or did we?

"We don't need any sleep, do we, Angel Dahl?"

Even though she didn't like that name, she smiled at me. "No, Mr. McLean, we don't. We're in New York.

And we have a mission to accomplish." She gazed up at the magnificent Rockefeller Center. We'd head out when the stores opened and buy some clothes. I'd get her whatever she wanted, though I knew that wouldn't be much.

We leaned over the gate. Happy couples swirled past in front of us, the sound of their blades cutting the ice and a recorded Christmas carol all we could hear. Angel stood very close to me. As we talked, we tried to take the information we had and make something out of it, make some decisions. We really couldn't go back to the hotel. John was still after us, and I had only a few days left to get my task done. We had to make some progress, *now*. But try as we might, we still couldn't figure anything out.

Then I thought of Leon. I didn't know why I hadn't considered contacting him before. Sure, it was about four in the morning, but he'd respond. I knew he would. He had a voice-activated iPhone with a touch screen that he could operate with a stylus he held in his mouth. He always kept his phone plugged in and by his bed. He'd answer, especially if he knew it was me.

"I have this friend," I told Angel. "He's got this muscle disease and he's in a wheelchair. He can't use his limbs much and…this disease, this IBM thing, it's going to kill him. But he's really smart. Really, really smart. I think he's a genius."

She smiled. "He's your friend?"

"Yeah, I help him out."

"You do?"

"Yeah, it's no big deal. My point is, he might be able to make something out of our clues. I'll text him."

"But it's the middle of the night."

"I know."

Q! I texted. We have a problem here in New York.

Ten seconds later, my phone pinged. NYC? Wow. Been talking to your boy Webb, helping him out. He's getting around too. Hey, you said "we"! Got a chick with u? Better not! Shirley is the best!

I know. Angel's just a friend.

Angel? Friend? Is that Bad Adam texting me or u?

He's the only person I've ever told about Bad Adam. Shirley doesn't even know. I especially don't want to tell her. It would scare her, and she might think I'm nuts.

Never mind that, Q. We have a problem for u to solve.

Shoot.

I imagined him in his room, lights out, lying there in his bed, unable to move much, the stylus in his mouth, happy to be talking with me. I often wondered what he thought about at night when the lights went out. I didn't have time to tell him every-thing that had happened in Bermuda. The whole Grandpa thing would blow him away. So I simply told him that we were searching for someone or something, we weren't sure which, but we were pretty sure it had something to do with spies, and all we had for clues were the letter *W*, which kept turning up, and a glass eye on a desk.

What kind of glass eye?

What did he mean by what kind? It was a glass eyeball! But then I remembered something strange about it. I thought of that first riveting moment in Grandpa's office in Paget. The iris on the eye...it was gold.

Had some gold on it, I texted.

Goldeneye! he immediately answered.

All I knew about *Goldeneye* was that it was the name of a James Bond movie, one with Pierce Brosnan as 007. It wasn't a particularly good one, done ages ago, in 1995. I'd only seen it once. I couldn't even remember much about it. Bad Adam recalled the Bond Girls, of course, especially Famke Janssen as Xenia Onatopp, who liked to kill men with her thighs during, shall we say, *romantic* moments. It was the first James Bond movie Brosnan did and the first one not taken directly from an Ian Fleming novel.

Thanks, Q. I think. I signed off.

As we walked away from 30 Rock, I was talking out loud about *Goldeneye*. Angel was kind of quiet, just letting me ramble on.

"Why would Grandpa be so into *Goldeneye*?"

"Mr. Know."

"Right, Mr. Know. Why would Mr. Know be so into it? It's just a Pierce Brosnan Bond flick."

"He was all right—better than Timothy Dalton."

"But why does Know have nothing on his desk but a golden eye?"

"Because it must mean a lot to him, a whole lot."

"*Goldeneye*? A lame Bond movie? It isn't even from a Fleming novel."

Angel stopped in her tracks. "It's more than that," she said.

I turned around.

"More than that?"

"I remember now. That movie was given that name for a specific reason."

"And that was?"

"Goldeneye is a place, a very important place."

"A place?"

"It's Ian Fleming's home in Jamaica. It's where he wrote all the Bond novels."

My heart leaped. "Really?"

"They filmed scenes for *Dr. No* around there. I read somewhere that it's a resort now."

I stood there thinking. Grandpa or Mr. Know knew Fleming. Angel had said that he talked about him all the time. He hated William Stephenson and loved Ian Fleming. I was willing to bet that something had happened down there in Jamaica, something traumatic, something that Grandpa was involved in. Or, at the very least, there was some secret there that might unravel all of this. I could just feel it. Goldeneye. He kept that eye to remember it by. Maybe the answers were there in the Caribbean? *W knows. W marked the spot.* That's what he often said into the mirror. Was the spot somewhere in that resort? I thought of our third clue—the Cuban Missile Crisis. Cuba was in the Caribbean too. I thought of *Dr. No,* of the scenes on the beach there, of the blue tropical waters and the heat. Then I thought of *Mr.* Know. We had the money and a couple of days. *Jamaica.*

"Ready for another plane ride?" I asked Angel Dahl.

TWELVE

ROADBLOCK

We had to get something to wear. As soon as the stores opened, we'd be in them. We walked around the city for a few hours, killing time, getting a bite to eat at a falafel stand, staring at everything. It was pretty cool. Angel told me a bit more about her life in Bermuda. She had tried to run away a few times, but really, where could she go? They looked after her needs at home. She had everything, materially, that her peers had, and sometimes more. But I wondered if she'd ever received a hug or much encouragement. She did fine in school and it was a good school, but she had few friends. She'd never had a boyfriend. She claimed she didn't want one. Mr. Know didn't talk to her often. When he did, he was usually critical. She knew she was a bit clumsy, but he would laugh at her anytime she bumped into anything. She liked to exercise in their basement fitness room. Whenever Know saw her in shorts, though, he'd say that her legs looked huge and laugh. So she worked out in sweats. She blurted that last bit out kind of angrily, then stopped talking, as if she'd revealed too much. It was hard to believe that Grandpa would say something like that. I turned the subject to shopping.

This was going to be interesting—buying clothes in New York with a girl. Shirley would have loved it. She isn't like many of the other girls in my school, who all have to have the latest thing, even if that latest thing looks incredibly stupid on them. And I'm not the sort of guy who cares that much about fashion either. I like to look a little trendy, if I can, but you won't see me with designer underwear showing about a mile above low-riding pants.

Despite my lack of enthusiasm, when Angel and I went shopping, I was definitely the one who was the most into it. Imagine that! And I barely even bothered to look at the labels or the price tags. I bought a pair of dark skinny jeans, a Sabres T-shirt, another *Skyfall* T-shirt and a warm Yankees sweatshirt. I also quietly grabbed some more of the undies I like and a few dark socks. She spotted that, smiled and said, "Good move!" She was much more interested in what I was buying than in her own stuff, which was extra weird for a girl. She even forced me to buy a nice white, long-sleeved shirt and a pair of black dress pants. "You're James Bond," she teased. "You have to look good."

Getting her to buy anything was like pulling teeth, and everything she got was baggy—a baggy pair of camo pants, a couple of baggy *I Love New York* T-shirts I knew I'd never even see on her because they'd be under the baggy gray sweatshirt she had on or the baggy brown sweater she'd gotten to keep warm. She wouldn't even model them, nor would she show me how she looked in the little black dress I absolutely made her buy. ("If I'm James Bond," I said, "then you have to be a Bond Girl." She glared at me.) She took everything into a change room, came back out and said, "Okay" and moved on. (Though, of course, she tripped once coming out.)

She hadn't done anything with her hair since I'd first seen her in Bermuda. It still looked uncombed and unfashionable, even a little dirty, though it was a nice auburn color with a bit of wave to it. She kept her blue eyes hidden behind her shades most of the time, though she sometimes wore awful horn-rimmed glasses once the sun went down. I figured we needed bathing suits for Jamaica, and I bought a pair of red, knee-length trunks, which she said would look great on me. But I had to insist that she get a suit herself. She said she didn't like bathing suits (which seemed pretty strange for a girl from Bermuda), and it was only after I said I wouldn't take her to Jamaica without one that she finally grabbed a boring-looking one-piece right off the rack, the kind a seventy-year-old woman would wear. I think it was brown, but it was hard to tell. She was really uncomfortable in the clothing stores, never looked at herself in the mirrors and was happy when we were finally finished.

"Does your girlfriend wear a bikini?" she asked when we left the last store.

"Yes," I said, almost as if to prove that it wasn't the end of the world. But Shirley didn't always wear them; she had a one-piece as well, and she usually chose that even though she looked great in the more revealing outfit—really great. And then, out of nowhere, an image of Vanessa Lincoln in her bikini shot through my mind. It was red, white and blue and very skimpy. I saw her wearing it at Crystal Beach last summer. She is, shall I say, full-figured. *She looked awesome,* said Bad Adam. *You know it.* But I banished the image instantly.

I bought Angel a prepaid cell phone (she didn't have one in Bermuda), we got new backpacks, and we were back at JFK Airport before noon. I kept peeking in the taxi's rearview mirror, hoping no one was following us. No one seemed to be. But if John was really on our trail again, I had the distinct feeling that we wouldn't even know it.

I felt nervous buying the tickets and even more so taking my Walther PPK through the special-baggage check. I had to go through a long chat with the officials again, even though I showed them the pass I'd been given at this very airport, the one that had allowed me to take the empty "collectible" gun back and forth from Bermuda.

I had toyed with the idea of getting some bullets for the gun when I was walking uptown toward Rockefeller Center. I was really worried about what John might do to us if he caught us again and wondered if I needed to protect myself (and especially Angel) in a serious way. I was sure I could get ammunition. I'd heard about guys my age buying bullets in gun shops around Buffalo. These guys, apparently, looked just a touch older than they were. They'd been asked for their IDs, but the shop owners hadn't even really looked at their faces—they'd just had them flash the IDs to make it legal. It didn't seem right.

I'd made that point in a big discussion about gun control we had in the cafeteria one day. Vanessa had been there. Her dad is a member of the National Rifle Association and a big supporter of our armed forces (I am too). She said everyone had a right to arm themselves, every last citizen in America; it was our right under the constitution. I was ashamed that I hadn't argued with her about that. I'd looked at the constitution myself, and the part that covered arming yourself seemed to be more about the military than citizens and was written over two hundred years ago, when people had muskets and lived in dangerous, outlying places, not in modern cities. Nor did they have anything remotely like today's assault rifles, which can fire off about a million rounds a second and tear someone to shreds. But that conversation had been about a year ago, before I went to France. I hadn't realized in those days what a dough-head Vanessa was. I guess beauty can blind you, if you don't watch it.

Anyway, I didn't get the bullets. I thought better of it. But I have to admit that it was exciting to think of firing the Walther PPK, and at first I'd even tried to convince myself that I'd get the bullets and just shoot a few off at a firing range or something. I also tried to tell myself that the *W* might indeed refer to the Walther and that using it would somehow tell me something more about the mystery I was pursuing. That was stupid. So was getting the bullets. It was like I had momentarily thought I was in the movies or a video game or an alternate universe. I think it was all Bad Adam's idea.

We sat in the lounge at JFK, trying to sleep despite it being almost noon, waiting for our flight to Jamaica. But both of us were unable to even close our eyes, excited but also very nervous, constantly glancing around for any sight of John. After a while, we forgot about him. That wasn't smart. A spy should always be vigilant. Always.

I had my phone out, looking at the Goldeneye resort website, trying to book a room for us online, putting it in Angel's name since she was eighteen. I had to use my credit card, but I didn't want to answer any questions about my age. It was a really high-end place and the rooms—little houses, really—were about a thousand dollars a shot. All I could afford was a one-bedroom "villa" (as they called it), and only for one night—we had to get in and out and solve things that fast. But all the villas, both the ones on the beach and on what was called the "lagoon," were taken. I shouldn't have been surprised. It was the Christmas holidays, after all, and here I was, on December 29, trying to book a room for that very evening. Even the Ian Fleming Villa was taken. I wondered what that was—it was incredibly expensive, so I couldn't have afforded it anyway. But what were we going to do if we couldn't get a room? They wouldn't let you into the resort without one. Would I have to break in? I had to go there. It was the only light at the end of my tunnel.

Frustrated, I took out a Jamaican tourist brochure I'd found in the airport lounge, put it on my knee and started writing out the clues we had, right on the brochure's surface, over and over—*Goldeneye, W, W marked the spot* and *Cuban Missile Crisis*. Then a shadow loomed over my shoulder. I looked across to the seat in front of me and saw Angel staring back, her eyes wide. She wasn't looking at me: she was staring up…at John.

"No one move," he said evenly. "Everyone just stay nice and quiet-like for a count of ten and then get up and proceed slowly over there, toward the window."

He was motioning to an area where no one else was sitting, a stretch of about ten or fifteen connected seats.

"We need to have a little chat." His voice sounded alarmingly calm.

I considered making a run for it. I looked at Angel and she looked back as if she were trying to see right into my brain. Could we make it? Was it a good idea to try? Could we lose him in the crowd? Were there any policemen nearby this time?

"Don't even think about it," John added.

I was worried he would do something that was not, shall we say, good for our health. Angel seemed to have decided that we should do as he said too.

That wasn't a good sign. She had known what to do last time. But now she just looked frightened. I tried not to be. I needed to protect her.

We got up and walked slowly to the vacant area. He made us sit beside each other, looking out the big airport windows at the planes on the tarmac. When he started to talk, he still seemed very calm. In fact, he was smiling. I quickly realized how smart that was—to any observer, we were friends having a nice friendly discussion. What others couldn't see was that his hand was on the gun inside a big pocket in his jacket, and the gun was pointed at us. It amazed me that he could do that with the weapon so easily, and that he looked so pleasant. That was terrifying. What was this guy capable of?

"Do you know what a silencer is?" he asked.

"Yes," said Angel before I could answer. "Technically, it's called a suppressor." Even in this tense moment, it sort of ticked me off that she knew that.

"Do you know that I could kill both of you right now with the weapon concealed in my jacket, the weapon with an attached suppressor, and that I have positioned you so that not only will no one hear the sound of the bullets entering your hearts and killing you instantly—and I will not miss—but when you slump over, no one in this lounge will see it? I need just a split second to eliminate you both and only a few more seconds to exit the area. I have connections here who will help me. I have connections everywhere."

"Everywhere?" I asked.

"How do you think I located you in New York? How do you think I found the hotel you were staying in? I believe it was rooms 1412 and 1413?"

"CIA?" I asked. I hoped he didn't see me gulp.

"MI6?" asked Angel.

"A little of one and a good deal of the other," he said, glancing around. "So you see," he added, smiling again but this time actually looking genuinely friendlier, "you have nothing to fear. I am with the good guys. Surely you aren't afraid of your own governments? I followed you simply to talk with you, and to bring Ms. Hicks home."

I glanced at Angel. Her eyes flashed up at me and then down to the floor. He didn't seem anything like a good guy.

"It's not my government," she said.

He ignored her comment.

"Mr. Murphy, please hand me that brochure."

He knew my real name. I gave him the brochure without thinking.

"Hmmm." He looked down at what I'd written on it. *Goldeneye, W, W marked the spot* and *Cuban Missile Crisis.* "What's this all about?"

Why had I written out our clues? I bet a real spy never would have done that.

"Nothing," said Angel, too quickly.

"Nothing? Do you have anything to add, Mr. Murphy?"

"No."

"Look, relax. I told you, I work for the good guys." He eyed us. We didn't say a word. There was silence for a long time. "What does this mean?" he asked again, and this time he didn't sound as friendly.

"I don't know," I said. "Honestly." And that was true, sort of. What I said reminded me of a line from *Adventures of Huckleberry Finn*, a great novel I'd read recently. It's really funny from the very first page, where Huck, who is an excellent character and kind of progressive in his views despite being a hick and living in the olden days, actually starts talking about the author who wrote the book he's in. It's amazing! He says the author likes to tell "stretchers" when he writes, "but mainly he told the truth." That cracked me up. Huck also said, "I never seen nobody but lied, one time or another."

Well, I suppose I was lying at that very moment, but "mainly" telling the truth. Maybe that's what spies do? Everyone in the John Le Carré novels was certainly a little fast and loose with the truth. Maybe you had to be that way to be in espionage. Maybe you had to be that way in life to survive, period. Was Le Carré saying that? I knew that Angel and I had to be careful with John, very careful. We couldn't tell him the whole truth.

"You don't know? Really?" he asked. I'd never seen anyone examine someone's face quite the way he did then. His gaze drilled into me, checking out my throat, my mouth, even my forehead and ears, as if he could spot something, some giveaway, some swallow or twitch.

"Yes!" said Angel, as if to divert his attention to her. "He's telling the truth."

"You, young lady, are going home."

"I'm not so young anymore, John."

"You're young enough, my dear. You are still Mr. Hicks's ward."

"I'm staying with Adam."

"Mr. Murphy is going home too."

"I am?"

"Yes, shortly. I have arranged your flight to Buffalo. It departs soon. Jim will be meeting Ms. Hicks at the Bermuda airport. Your flight, my dear, will depart late this afternoon."

"Aren't you coming with me?"

"No."

I detected a slight pause before he answered, very brief, yet definitely there. And I noticed a quick swallow too, barely evident. Maybe I was learning how to be a spy, how to play the game. I had been so suspicious about so many things over the last day or two that it was becoming second nature to try to "read" people. I wondered if John was telling a "stretcher," just "mainly" the truth. And if so, why? What was he hiding?

We didn't talk for a few moments. Angel kept looking over at me. It seemed like she was about to cry. I couldn't look back. My mind was racing. I *had* to help her, and I *had* to know more about Grandpa.

I couldn't give up. I had risked life and limb to get this far, and so had Angel, who was desperate to have her freedom and discover who she was. I couldn't go through life thinking that Grandpa had deceived me and the whole McLean family so horribly, even if he did it for all the right reasons. All I would have left was the Walther PPK, and even it might be lost, since it was on its way to Jamaica and I might never get it back.

"Your bag will be retrieved for you and will make its way to Buffalo as well." These guys were mind readers extraordinaire. Well, at least I'd have the gun. But that wasn't good enough, far from it.

"He isn't Mr. Hicks," I said sternly to John, without even looking at him. Maybe I could get him talking.

"What's that?"

"The man you work for is David McLean. He's my grandfather."

John smiled. It didn't seem like a revelation to him or even a strange thing to say. I wished it had. "Guy Hicks, David McLean, Mr. Know...it doesn't matter what he calls himself. I am an operative. I work for the good guys; I do what is right. You will have to satisfy yourself with that. But if I ever see you in Bermuda again, I am sorry to say that you will be eliminated. There is a greater good at stake. I am sure your grandfather, whoever he is and wherever he is, would understand that." He smiled again. "Knowing him, I am sure of that."

I didn't like the sound of that either.

"I'll come back," I muttered.

He turned his face toward me. "Look at me," he said.

I've heard about "cold eyes" or "dead eyes," the ones that crime writers often say bad guys and murderers have. Like Goldfinger, or Javier Bardem in *Skyfall* when he took out the dentures that were holding his face together and his cheeks collapsed on-screen, or the arch-villain Le Chiffre in *Casino Royale* when he had Daniel Craig strapped naked to a chair and was torturing him. Well, John had those kind of eyes at this very moment. It actually made me shiver.

"No, you won't," he said.

He didn't swallow at all. Nothing on his face moved. I knew right then that I couldn't go back to Bermuda. I had to think of something else.

"Before I see you off"— he smiled —"I want to explore the things you wrote on this brochure, Mr. Murphy. It was brave of you to say that you knew nothing about them, but you do."

"He doesn't," said Angel.

"Quiet, Ms. Hicks." He gave her a cold look and turned back to me again. He didn't have the dead eyes now, but they weren't entirely friendly either; it was a bland expression with a threat inside it. "Care to explain, Adam?"

"No," I said.

"Well, let's do an exchange then, shall we?"

"What do you mean?"

"You give me something and I'll give you something. It's really quite fair and equitable, given that I could simply kill you."

There was a long pause.

"Goldeneye is in Jamaica," I said.

"Very good. It is Ian Fleming's old home, isn't it? Now a resort? You know all that, don't you?"

"Yes."

"You won't be going there either," he said.

"All right." I said it straight to his face, without moving a muscle.

"We have people there as well, of course. They would make things decidedly unpleasant for you and for anyone who accompanied you." He looked at Angel again.

But I had seen him swallow, slightly. Had he just told a stretcher? And if so, what did it mean? I glanced at Angel, who looked my way for an instant when John turned back to me. She smiled, ever so slightly. Then the smile vanished.

Goldeneye, I thought. There really is something there.

"I said I would give you something too, and I am a man of my word." He paused and thought for a moment, looking away, then turned back to me. "Mr. Know indeed had something to do with the Cuban Missile Crisis. He was there in 1962, deeply involved. That is a tidbit that will take you nowhere. In other words, it's a nice fact for a civilian to possess."

Within an hour, I was on a flight to Buffalo and Angel was on her way to Bermuda. We didn't say goodbye. We didn't have to. We hoped to meet again, and soon.

THIRTEEN

BOND ISLAND

I knew how I was going to get to Jamaica. It was simple. When John swallowed, it had told me he was lying when he said there were people at Goldeneye who would watch me and kill me if I ever showed up there. At least, I hoped that was what it meant. There was a secret here that John was hiding, maybe a secret inside a secret. A spy among spies?

I knew that I could simply get off the plane in Buffalo and board one back to Jamaica. I'd take a different route this time—Chicago first, then the Caribbean. But was I running out of time? I had just two days left! And just one in Jamaica.

More important, was I right about John? If not, lethal people would be waiting for me on that island, and I was a dead man. A *dead* man! This was no movie. Suddenly, I wondered if it was all worth it. But I had to know about Grandpa. I just had to. He had taught all of us to be brave, and I was going to be brave now.

But what about Angel? What if things didn't work out? Would I never see her again? I kept wondering if she had sacrificed our relationship—friendship was a better way to put it—for me, for my pursuit of the truth about my grandfather. I was worried that she was obediently going back to that awful house in Paget Parish in order to make it look like we were both defeated when she knew from that glance we'd exchanged that I was on my way to Jamaica. What if she couldn't get away? Would I be able to accomplish whatever I needed to accomplish without her by my side? She had been an amazing companion, smart and spy-like, and a kind person to boot.

And even when I did get to Jamaica, what would I be able to do? I had so little to go on: the Cuban Missile Crisis and *W marked the spot* and then, of course, the *W* itself. I still didn't have even the remotest idea what those things meant. And I had so little time!

Before I'd departed New York, I had texted Shirley. John was sitting nearby, watching.

Hi sweetheart, looking forward to seeing you, just another two days, can't wait!

I couldn't tell her exactly what was going on. Not yet. I would, after I got home. I told Shirley everything these days. It was the best policy. I'd tell her about Angel too. She'd be cool with that. She was pretty secure. I'd just say that Angel was a nice girl, attractive as a person and that was it. That was the truth, wasn't it? I didn't think it was a stretcher.

I thought I'd hear from Shirley right away. But I didn't.

Instead, I spent the flight to Buffalo thinking about the clues, still getting nowhere. When we landed, I booked a flight to Chicago and found a seat in the departures lounge where I could keep my back to the wall. That's what I'd read spies do: keep everything in front of them so they can't be taken by surprise. I also didn't want to run into my dad. He flew out of this airport all the time, and meeting up with him would wreck everything. I'd have to make up a real stretcher to explain my situation to him—a stretcher in the name of doing the right thing, of course.

I texted Leon.

Hey, Q, I'm in Buffalo.

He answered immediately. Cool, James, I'm on my way! I'll get Mom to bring me over.

No, I'm not home. I'm at the airport.

Like I said, on my way.

No, don't come to the airport! I'll be gone by the time u get here.

Gone?

To Chicago.

Chi town!

Then Jamaica.

Goldeneye?

U got it.

Ah! Solving things?

No. Got questions for u.

Shoot, A-Murph.

Need to know what "W" might mean and "W marked the spot" and more about the Cuban Missile Crisis. Can u help me out with the way the last one connects to spies?

Likely.

Know lots about it?

Definitely.

Ever hear of a guy named Guy Hicks and if he had anything to do with it?

No, will check, text when I know something.

A text came in from Shirley shortly after that. Sounds exciting, was all it said.

My flight to Chicago was delayed, which was super frustrating. I paced around, wasting hours, waiting to hear the announcement that the plane was ready. I'd only been checking texts from Leon and Shirley, so now I took a look at the others. I couldn't believe what my cousins were telling me. Spencer was running around Toronto on the trail of something pretty bizarre and Bunny, now without a cell and incommunicado, had disappeared. DJ was in London with no time to talk, pursuing secret codes. Steve sounded intense and in love in exotic Spain, and Rennie had somehow found his way from South America to an even more dangerous place, Detroit. Webb just said, in the US, which was almost as ominous as all of the other messages put together. It sounded evasive. But I couldn't worry about those guys. I had too much on my plate. I had to get to Jamaica as soon as possible.

Finally, I boarded an evening flight, no Dad yet in sight. I'd been to Chicago once, and it was a very cool city too, right up there with New York and Toronto, but I would only see the airport this time.

O'Hare International Airport is huge. In fact, I think it's one of the biggest in the world. I raced around looking for the next flight to Jamaica, eyes alert for anyone who might be following me. But it was late by then, and the first flight I could get to the Caribbean left at about three in the morning. I didn't care. I got my luggage and "collectible" gun through customs and then slept for a while in the departures lounge, right near the exit to the plane so they'd rouse me if I was sleeping when my flight was ready to board.

I woke up about forty-five minutes before departure, almost jumping to my feet, obviously on edge. I turned on my phone and went to the Goldeneye site again. I'd been on it about fifty times since JFK, trying to book a room, with no luck. Now, when I tried again, bingo! There was one available. Someone had canceled. And just for tomorrow night! I booked it and then got up and started to pace, absolutely pumped.

But I still hadn't heard back from Leon. If he couldn't find a connection between Guy Hicks and the Cuban Missile Crisis, then no one could. His lack of response wasn't a good thing—sure I had a place at Goldeneye, but I was heading down to Jamaica without a single thing to work with, and the clock was ticking fast.

My first thoughts—in fact, almost all my thoughts—in the darkness on the flight south were about Angel. I wondered what she was planning. Or was she planning anything at all? She likely had no choice but to go home to Paget and stay there until she was able to fly the coop. But would she ever be able to? Did they intend her harm? I hated to think about that, especially given my grandfather's central role in all of this. But I comforted myself by remembering that John had assured us he was with the "good guys," and he certainly did seem to have access to classified information through some sort of powerful organization. It couldn't be a crime syndicate or anything like that; it had to be a group like the CIA or MI6, with its hands on government sources, with information about private citizens. Otherwise, how would he have been able to find us in New York? But then I wondered if a highly organized criminal connected to the mob or some other group might actually be able to do the same. That really gave me the shivers, given that I was flying away from Angel toward Jamaica. She was a young woman who might be in peril, and I wasn't being much of a hero.

I thought about what had happened just before John had taken me to my flight to Buffalo. He had demanded Angel's backpack and gone through it thoroughly. And I mean *thoroughly*. He had examined every inch of it and even checked to make sure there was nothing sewn into the lining. He found her passport but didn't confiscate it. She'd need it to get through customs in Bermuda. Then he made her stand up, and he frisked her. He did it really fast, keeping his hands away from areas that were inappropriate. He did the whole thing in an instant and with his back to me and I didn't see Angel after that. I doubted he'd care about her new cell, if he found it. With her on a plane, and us so far away from each other anyway, it was useless to her now.

But I was hoping he had missed something else, something in particular.

The sun started coming up as the plane descended over the Caribbean. I could see the Florida Keys. Then we went out over the water, descending slightly, and I could actually spot some boats, ones that must have been awfully big to be spied from tens of thousands of feet in the air. They were probably luxury cruise liners, which made me think of Mom and my aunts. Maybe they were actually in one of those boats. Man, would Mom be blown away if she knew what I was doing.

We continued our descent. Beneath us a huge island came into view. I immediately knew what it was. Cuba. It didn't look so awful from up here, sitting there in the blue water between America and Jamaica.

Most Americans hate it. Or at least we are supposed to. It is considered a very un-American place, the land of communism and bad old Fidel Castro in our backyard. Many folks have fled from Cuba over the years to get to our "land of the free and home of the brave," some taking deadly chances on little boats and life rafts to brave the waters of the Caribbean to get to Florida and freedom. Or at least that's how most of us like to see it. My Canadian cousins, the few who have actually been there on vacations since Canadians have no problems with Cuba at all, said it was a beautiful place, with political issues, yes, and poverty, but no more so than any other Central American country. They also claimed it had better health care than America (though they said "the US," of course). I didn't know how to feel about the whole thing. Dad was a Democrat and Mom was a left-wing Democrat (in other words, a Canadian), and they liked the idea of universal health care and didn't hold strong views about Cuba. They said they hoped that someday America would make its peace with Cuba and we could all go down there on a trip.

But the Cuban Missile Crisis itself was a whole other story. I'd learned a bit about it in school, but I had googled it in New York and again while I waited in Chicago. I found some interesting things. It would have been difficult to find a single American who had good thoughts about Cuba in 1962. That was right in the middle of the Cold War, when the evil Soviet Union and America were almost daily threatening to blow each other up. Both superpowers had the bombs to do it. Spies were everywhere in those days. James Bond was about to spring off Ian Fleming's pages and onto the big screen and make a huge impact. Everyone west of the Berlin Wall knew that the bad guys in those films were always the ones with the Russian accents. They were always *seriously* bad dudes and often nuts, bent on world domination. The year before the missile crisis, America had been so desperate to destroy the commie menace in Cuba that they supported the CIA's attempt to invade the island at a place called the Bay of Pigs. We lost. We don't like losing. Then, our secret service spotted big Soviet missiles on the ground in Cuba, right next to us, pointed in our direction. President Kennedy just about had a fit. He told Khrushchev to either get rid of them or it was war, and Khrushchev said if we tried to make him it was war. Their sort of war could easily have meant world destruction—the biggest confrontation of all time. It would have made World War II look like a tea party. Our armed forces went on high alert all over the world. People were stocking up on food, preparing to live in bomb shelters and thinking about killing themselves before the bombs got them. It's hard to imagine now.

But how was Grandpa—or Guy Hicks or Mr. Know—connected to all of that? John had actually said that Know had been involved.

There was no *W* in *Cuba* or *Missile* or *Crisis.*

As we flew over Cuba toward Jamaica, I could actually see some of the roads and buildings and the countryside from the air. It looked green and beautiful.

Rather than going to Kingston, which was Jamaica's capital and biggest city, I was flying into Montego Bay. Montego was on the north shore, where the Goldeneye resort was, facing the sea. Once I landed, I wouldn't have to make my way through heavy traffic to get where I was going. The airport was just east of the town, in the direction of the resort. I could find transportation and start moving. Time was of the essence.

I stared down at Jamaica as we began our final descent. It was about seven in the morning, and people were beginning to move about down there, starting their day. Wikipedia said Jamaica had one of the highest crime rates in the world and lots of problems with poverty. But it also had some awfully rich people and big businesses, and lots of travelers said it was the most beautiful place on earth. (I guess that's why Ian Fleming lived there when he wasn't in London—he liked beautiful places and beautiful women.) Jamaica was home to the late Bob Marley, Mom's favorite musician, just about the coolest guy who ever lived. She had lots of Marley CDs and even videos of him performing. I looked down at the deep-green grasses and palm trees, the beaches and the blue water, and at the colorful homes and clothing so bright I could actually pick it out from above. I heard reggae music in my head and saw images of Marley dancing, his dreadlocks swirling in the air, that radiant smile on his face, the bass pumping like rolling thunder.

But I wasn't going anywhere that directly reminded me of the reggae king and his gritty reality, nor would it be much like the colorful streets of Montego Bay beneath me. My destination was a couple of hours away on this resort-filled northern coast: Goldeneye, where Ian Fleming had gone every time he wanted to write a Bond novel, where he lived during those exciting days in the early sixties, in that intense Cold

War era. The resort was built around his old place. It was as expensive and romantic as any tourist attraction on the island, and that was saying something.

I couldn't believe the blast of hot air that hit me when I walked out of the air-conditioned terminal. It was like being in a sauna, even at eight o'clock in the morning and less than forty-eight hours before New Year's Eve. The taxi and transit area was noisy, filled with people hawking things, yelling for passengers, no one shy and everyone dressed in the most colorful clothes this side of Miami Beach. The Goldeneye website had said I could get a shuttle out to the resort, and I saw it almost immediately. It occupied a central place in the lineup and was painted bright white with the resort name on the side; it looked to be about half full when I boarded.

I made my way toward the back. I was missing Angel, and it struck me that sitting toward the rear of the vehicle would be the sort of thing she would do. So I did too. A small passenger was trudging along in front of me and took a place behind me. I threw myself onto my seat and moved over to the window.

I had both seats to myself, with my backpack on the rack above me. I was going to try to enjoy the scenery on the way out, even though I knew I had just one day to solve everything. I glanced over my shoulder. That other passenger was directly behind me, also sitting alone and looking down at a book. All I could see was the top of a black-ballcapped head.

My thoughts kept returning to Angel. I was glad that I had given her a substantial amount of money. She didn't have a credit card, and she would have no chance of ever slipping away from Jim and getting out of Bermuda without cash. Even with cash, that chance was absolutely minimal. And yet, when John frisked her, he hadn't seemed to find the money. Or did he?

"You know," said the person behind me, "the flight from Bermuda to here is much faster than anything you can get from the US. I've been waiting for you for a while. What took you so long?"

It was Angel. *Angel Dahl!*

I turned around and almost leaped over the seat. She was sitting there smiling at me, wearing her trademark shades. She had slipped onto the shuttle and assumed the color of the seats! I calmed myself, but she sprang to her feet and slid in right beside me, her eyes sparkling over the tops of her shades and through her unkempt hair, our legs touching. She had that look girls get when they want to kiss you. Shirley often gets it, and it makes me feel great, really loved. *Shirley,* I thought. I love Shirley.

"Oh, Angel," I said, "it's good to see you."

"Yeah," she said, her voice losing a bit of its excitement, "it's good to see you too."

"I got us a reservation at Goldeneye."

Her smile returned.

"I knew you would, Mr. McLean."

"You did?" She seemed to have so much confidence in me, even more than Shirley did. Sometimes, Shirley could be a little critical. "So, what happened with you?"

She grinned again.

"Enter Angel Dahl, sitting in her seat on an American Airlines flight from New York to Bermuda, John-less."

"I can see it now."

"Enter her seatmates: a girl of about ten and her mother, coming home after visiting friends on the mainland for the Christmas holidays."

"Got you."

"Note the hat on the little girl's head, an old-fash-ioned, wide straw hat that's too big for her and tied around the chin with a ribbon. Note also her strange-looking sunglasses. Now, observe Angel Dahl—"

"Perhaps you should say the beautiful Angel Dahl? Isn't this supposed to be a dramatic story?"

"Yeah, but let's not stretch things too much." She sighed. "Observe Angel Dahl making a deal with the little girl, trading one of her *I ♥ NY* T-shirts for the oversized straw hat, and her own shades for the little girl's big wide ones."

"Yes?"

"Then, observe Angel Dahl slipping into the washroom before the plane lands and getting her black dress out of her bag and putting it on."

"You put on the little black dress? The one I got you to buy?" Bad Adam couldn't help but wonder what she looked like in it.

"Yes…except I didn't buy the one you wanted me to. I took another one off a rack when you weren't looking."

"You did?"

She could see my disappointment and looked a little guilty. "Adam, it just wasn't me."

"So, what is this one like?"

The shuttle pulled out. She was sitting there beside me in her baggy sweatpants and baggy sweatshirt, so she'd taken the dress off again on the way to Jamaica.

"Well, it isn't exactly formfitting."

"What a surprise."

"No, it's long and has long sleeves and a high neck and is very loose and comfortable."

"Comfortable? So, you're telling me it looks like a black potato sack?"

She scrunched up her face. "Yeah, kind of."

I frowned. "On with the story."

"Enter Angel Dahl getting off the plane at L.F. Wade International Airport with the straw hat pulled down over her face, hair tied up under it, the little girl's big shades on, wearing the unusual long black dress with the turtleneck pulled up over her chin, using a spy technique she learned from a book about William Stephenson to make herself seem shorter than she really is. It is in the way you walk. Observe Angel Dahl assuming the color of the wall, stepping right past Jim, who is waiting in the arrivals area.

All she needs is a few seconds. Observe Angel Dahl making a beeline to the escalators, rushing over to Departures, hustling to the check-out counters for international flights, booking the next one to Jamaica, which was departing very soon since there are many flights between the islands. Oh, and observe Ms. Dahl buying herself a new pair of shades."

"And," I said, "observe her boarding a flight to Montego Bay, Jamaica, rushing out of the airport and sneaking onto the shuttle to the Goldeneye Resort before the so-called Adam McLean even sees her."

"The devilishly handsome Adam McLean."

"Now you are really stretching things."

"No, I'm not."

She gave me a long look when she said that. It felt kind of awkward. Angel was kind of awkward, period, exactly what you'd expect of someone who hadn't spent a lot of time interacting with people. But there was something about her that was so genuine too.

"I got here long before you, late last night. I had to sleep in the arrivals lounge. I saw you get off the flight and trailed you. You didn't even notice me! I got in front of you and onto the shuttle. I saw some girls eyeing you."

"Let's think about what we have to do next," I said quickly. "We don't have any time to lose."

But then a bad thought came into my mind. Something wasn't right about her story. How did Angel Dahl *really* get on that flight from Bermuda to Jamaica? I remembered again that she wasn't allowed a credit card. Back home, she was given money when she needed it. She had what she wanted, but only when she asked. I had given her quite a bit of cash in New York, but John had frisked her at the airport, so how did she pay for the plane ride? When I thought about it again, it was hard to believe he hadn't found her money. I had to ask her straight out. I wasn't going to Goldeneye with her if she was working for the other side.

"How did you pay for the flight?" I said bluntly.

"With the money you gave me."

"But—"

"Yeah, John frisked me. But he didn't find it."

"But that's almost impossible."

"Not for a woman." She smiled.

"A woman?"

"Yes," she sighed. "Uh, that's what I am, Adam." She looked a little miffed.

"Yeah, of course, I uh, I didn't mean—"

"My bra."

"Excuse me?"

"I put the money in my bra." She gave me a self-satisfied grin.

I remembered then that John hadn't wanted to touch her anywhere that would look creepy, not in public in the airport. She had put the money in the one place he wouldn't dare search. She'd probably somehow transferred it there when he wasn't looking. He had no idea how clever she was.

Not a big area to hide money, said Bad Adam to me. *Surprised it didn't slip right through and land on the floor.*

Shut up! I shouted at him inside my head. I wanted to punch his lights out.

"You're brilliant," I told her. She grinned.

It was now December 30, zero eight hundred hours. We had one day and night at Goldeneye. I had to be back in Buffalo by the next night. Mom would be flying home then. *Tomorrow!* I couldn't believe it. There's a James Bond movie called *Tomorrow Never Dies*. I wished that was true.

We had to think of what we'd do the minute we got to the resort. But once the bus was rolling out of the airport and moving across Highway A1 along the northern coast, it was hard not to be distracted by the passing scenery. The shuttle was one of those tourist ones with massive windows that went almost floor to ceiling, so you could see as much as possible of the outdoors. And what an outdoors!

It wasn't that it was perfect out there. There was lots of poverty. But even the few ramshackle houses and huts, the tough-looking men, the poor women, kids in bare feet, the dirt roads, were set in an absolute paradise. It was the most colorful place I'd ever seen, as if God had put some sort of lens over it to make everything look bright, bursting with the most radiant hues on earth. Jamaica was green, very green, but also yellow and red and purple and all the other colors of the rainbow. The air smelled salty. As we moved out of the suburban part of Montego Bay and into the countryside, I spotted jerk-chicken restaurants and little clubs and bars with Red Stripe beer advertised outside. Reggae music just pounded out the doors, even at this hour of the morning. It was *real* reggae music, from the land where it was born. Marley's image rose up on billboards and across T-shirts everywhere. Men had dreadlocks down to their waists, and women wore skimpy clothes in vividly colored fabrics.

The driver was talking about Jamaican history and I wanted to listen, but I couldn't concentrate. I asked Angel if she had come up with any ideas on her flight, but she shook her head. I wanted to will the shuttle forward, zip it along to Goldeneye in a flash. But the driver moved us slowly, so slowly. That was the pace of things in Jamaica. The people walking along looked like they were barely shuffling. Actually, it seemed like the right way to do things, the way the world should move. *But not today!*

As we traveled next to the Caribbean, a short gray stone wall appeared between us and the water, weathered and only a few feet high. Beyond it was not only an endless stretch of deep blue, but also, unseen in the distance, the other islands of the West Indies. It occurred to me that I must be looking directly toward Cuba's southern shore. In fact, if we were to sail straight out, I'd likely land near Guantanamo Bay, a piece of land in Cuba that America owned, the site of a famous military prison that was important during the missile crisis and today held the terrorists who wanted to attack and destroy our country.

It was a kind of symbol of America's modern Cold War. It held not only enemy soldiers and terrorists, but probably some spies who hated us and plotted against us, many of them put there by our own spies. There were lots of rumors that torture went on there. I didn't know whether to salute it or wish it didn't exist.

Soon we passed the old town of Falmouth, a picturesque place that likely didn't look much different when pirates were the rogue kings of the Caribbean three or four centuries ago. Then we passed Discovery Bay, where Christopher Columbus supposedly first set foot on the island. It was pretty incredible, but I barely looked at it and hardly heard the driver's travelogue.

W.

W marked the spot.

The Cuban Missile Crisis.

Just one day.

FOURTEEN

GOLDENEYE

We began passing resorts, many with famous names—
like Sandals and Club Med—that I'd seen in slick
magazine ads and on TV back home. You could see
their gates from the bus, and their beautiful hotels,
swimming pools, tennis courts and beaches beyond.
I wanted to pull the driver out of his seat, take his place
and press my foot down hard on the gas. I had a tourist
map on my knee, which was bouncing up and down
with my nervous twitch. I knew we were getting close.

Ten or fifteen minutes later I saw the big blue
sign for the little Ian Fleming Airport. I'd noticed
it on the map, just minutes from Goldeneye, but it

was amazing to see it in person. The creator of 007 had been in this very place! And, maybe, so had my grandfather. Had they plotted to help save the world right here during the Cuban Missile Crisis? Did they slip over to Cuba from these shores on inflatable boats, silently sneaking into that forbidding communist stronghold at night in black wet suits, real secret agents bearing Walther PPKs complete with suppressors? Did W send them? William Stephenson?

We passed Marley Beach and Reggae Beach and were told that James Bond Beach was nearby. We were *really* close. I thought of *Dr. No* being filmed here, with Sean Connery and his stunning Bond Girl both in bathing suits, one of the most iconic movie scenes of all time.

Goldeneye appeared moments later. We swept through the ornate gates and up to the front door of the beautiful two-story white building where guests checked in. Men in white jackets and shorts stood on the steps, holding small hot towels on shining silver plates for us to wipe our faces. I'd given Angel the window seat on the shuttle, and she had her face pressed up against the glass, looking very happy indeed. She smiled at me and took my hand as we got up to leave the bus. I let go as soon as we stepped down.

Everything was taken care of. A man took our bags. The Walther PPK was in mine, but I let him have it. All we had to do was show our identification and we would be taken to our accommodations.

"I, uh, had to book a one-bedroom villa. It was all that was available, and all I could afford," I told Angel as we waited to be taken to our room. I felt really bad about that and had been putting off telling her. I wouldn't have blamed her if she'd slapped me.

She blushed. "Not to worry," she said and smiled again.

What did that mean? I *was* worried. If Shirley found out about this, she'd be furious. And I wouldn't blame her, not one bit. I wanted to tell Angel right away that I'd sleep outside if necessary, but I couldn't because our attendant had come back and we wanted to make the resort people think we were a couple. We had to be convincing. She even took my hand again, though she snickered a bit when she did, as if it was an inside joke. I didn't give Bad Adam a chance to be excited about any of this. I cut him off before he could offer up a single thought; given his shallow views on Angel's looks, though, he might not have been too thrilled by the situation anyway.

The resort was incredibly beautiful. We walked along a narrow wooden bridge that went over a lagoon where other tourists were paddle-boating and swimming. Couples walked hand in hand along the private beach up ahead, kids in the water cried out with joy, you could hear gentle music playing, and alluring aromas of spicy food filled the air, mingling with the smell of the salty sea.

Once the resort guy had opened up our villa and snapped back all the shutters, he handed "Mr. Murphy" the key and left, and I started into my full apology.

"Angel, I am really sorry about this. I'll put some of the pillows on the floor and sleep in the bathroom or out on the—"

"Yeah," she said, "never mind—we'll work it out." She said it in a kind of dreamy voice as she gazed around at her surroundings. I could understand why. The place was stunning. It was on the beach, a curving, gorgeous stretch of white sand in front of transparent pale blue water. White umbrellas stood over tables that dotted the sand, and an infinity pool, as crystal-clear as the warm water, seemed to hang out into the sea. Our front door opened right onto the beach. Our little building was almost like a Jamaican chalet, with a gray shingled roof that looked thatched from a distance and white exterior walls. We had our own deck with sun chairs, and an outdoor shower was just out of sight among the vines and flowers. Inside, the walls were cool and white, and the bed (which made me gulp) was huge and decorated with colorful pillows. You reached it by walking up a short flight of wooden stairs onto a light-carpeted floor. Angel kicked off her flip-flops. We had an en suite bath-room, a desk for writing and huge open windows looking out over the sea. There was a bottle of cham-pagne on ice sitting on our gleaming wooden table. I had tried drinking a bit of alcohol a few times but hadn't touched a drop since I'd come back from France. I didn't think Angel would either. She didn't seem like that kind of girl.

She looked so happy, I thought she might cry. I hoped not. I would have no idea what to do.

"We have to get to work," I said.

"Right." She fell onto the bed, giggling. "Work."

FIFTEEN

ARMED AND DANGEROUS

"I'm starving," said Angel, sitting up on the bed a few minutes later.

"Okay, we can talk in the restaurant. Are you changing?"

She shook her head. She was going to stay in those sweats and that sweatshirt? In a beach resort?

It had been air-conditioned on the shuttle, so I'd left my long-sleeved Yankees shirt on. Now I pulled it off over my head. As I did, my *Skyfall* T pulled up too, so there I was, shirtless in front of her again. She didn't look away. I pulled it down.

"Let's go."

There were two eateries at the resort. The Gazebo, a cool, tree-house kind of restaurant that looked out over the sea, and another spot called the Bizot Bar, which had a great view too, but was more of a burger-and-fries place. We wanted something quick, so we headed to the Bizot. We both got some spicy jerk chicken and sweet-potato fries, washing it all down with a fruit drink that had actual fruit in it, served in a tumbler about a foot high with lots of ice and a tiny umbrella. We sat on the porch overlooking the beach, hearing the sounds of the sea and people enjoying themselves. I should have been beside myself with joy, but I was looking around, wondering what *W* meant and how it might be connected to this heaven on earth. Nothing was evident. Ian Fleming, I thought—it might have something to do with him. Angel and I gazed out over the water, viewing the scene from behind our dark shades.

My cell phone pinged.

Q here.

Yes?

Got some news for you, Bond, big news.

My heart rate increased. I pulled my chair closer to Angel and showed her the screen. She looked down at it, gasped and bent closer to the phone; our cheeks were almost touching.

Really?

I found an American spy named Stanley Shick on this list of operatives that some spy geek has collected. Shick was very active in the early 1960s, CIA, international espionage.

So?

Take a closer look at his last name.

I glanced at Angel. "Shick?" I said to her, puzzled. Then I started moving the letters around. Angel must have done the same. "Hicks!" she cried out. I texted the name back to my little buddy.

Bingo, wrote Leon. Most spies had cryptonyms or code names. Stanley Shick's was Guy.

"Guy Hicks!" whispered Angel.

"Wow!" I said out loud. "It's him!"

A man had just sat down near us, alone at a table. He looked over at us and smiled.

He disappeared, Leon texted. Last seen September 1962.

The month before the Cuban Missile Crisis.

Thanks a million, Q. I'll debrief you when I get home.

We are waiting for you. And when I say we, you know who I mean.

I set the phone down and noticed a slightly disgruntled look on Angel's face. She hadn't liked Leon's last sentence, but I wasn't thinking about that.

"Guy Hicks vanished on the eve of the Cuban Missile Crisis!" I exclaimed as quietly as possible.

"He must have been eliminated," said Angel.

"If that's true, then who is in the house in Bermuda?"

"Adam, don't jump to conclusions." But her eyes looked worried.

"Grandpa," I said.

"Don't—"

"Grandpa took his name. He took his place too! It *is* him. It's *his* scent on his shirts! Explain that!"

"But why would he take his place?"

I wasn't listening. I felt like crying. *Grandpa!*

"Excuse me," we heard someone say.

It was sometime between ten and eleven in the morning, so there was hardly anyone else in the bar, just us and the man who had come in after us and fitted himself into one of the wooden chairs at a table right next to us. I say "fitted" because he was, uh, a little heavy. Okay, he was fat, but there isn't anything wrong with that, as long as you are healthy. Problem was, he didn't look too fit. He was maybe sixty years old, with straggly, thinning hair poking out from under a truly ugly *I ♥ Jamaica* hat that looked like a really cheap knockoff of a Tilley hat. He was wearing awful red jean shorts that showed his very white, stubbly, thick legs, and hard black shoes and black socks, the socks pulled up almost to his knees. On his substantial upper body he sported an ugly beach shirt with flamingos and flowers and bikini-clad women on it. But under it, he wore something that caught my eye—the same *Skyfall* T-shirt that I had on, though his stretched over two or three pretty hefty rolls of flab. I wasn't judging him. He was likely a very nice man.

"Yes, sir?"

"I noticed your T-shirt, young fellow."

He had sort of a squeaky voice and a slight lisp. He squinted because he wasn't wearing shades. His glasses were thick, and each lens was circular and about the size of a grapefruit or bigger. He looked like a portly, balding owl.

"Yes," I said, "*Skyfall*. Great film."

"Indeed. Are you kids from America?" He had an American accent himself. I couldn't place it, but it sounded vaguely southern.

"Well, I am, but—"

"I am too," said Angel quickly. She'd dropped her Bermudian accent instantly. Maybe she'd learned how to talk like an American from watching TV. It was startlingly—almost suspiciously—good.

"I'm from the great state of Tennessee," he said with pride.

"We're from Buffalo. He's Leon and I'm Shirley," said Angel, her accent flat. Wow, she was clever. Do Americans really sound like that?

"Well, nice to meet you. I'm Homer Johnson."

"Hello, Mr. Johnson." I wanted to get back to Leon's incredible information. How could I make Homer go away?

"Ring a bell?"

"Excuse me?"

"Well, I am guessing you are a James Bond fan."

"I suppose I am, a little bit."

"Well, Homer Johnson is a little bit too."

Mr. Johnson was indeed more than a little bit. I bit my tongue to keep from laughing. "More than a little bit of what, sir?"

"I am the world's foremost expert on James Bond, if I may say so myself. Check it out. Homerjohnson007.com. That's why I come here. I visit every year and stay in the Ian Fleming Villa. That's where he actually lived, you know. It's the most expensive place in the resort, but not a problem for Homer Johnson. Yours truly was a legend in the toilet-seat industry, you know. I ran four factories back home in my day. Johnson Toilet Seats—*Sit on a Johnson and you'll feel like royalty!*"

I tried to ignore that. I also hate it when people refer to themselves in the third person, using their full names. But he seemed harmless, and lonely too. I imagined him prowling the resort every year, looking for people to impress with his 007 knowledge. Who knew how much of that he really had? He probably came here year after year just for that. It was kind of sad. He was also checking out Angel, which was kind of weird. She was a great girl, a really great girl, but not the sort guys check out. But this guy was going right at it. I had the sense that back in Bermuda,

Angel really struggled to get along with people, but ever since we'd been on the road together, she was her true self. She smiled at people, even strangers. She was doing that now with Homer Johnson, and he was eating it up.

"You should pop by the Ian Fleming House and I'll give you a tour."

"Sorry," I said. "We're kind of busy." I turned back to my phone, anxious to put the new facts together with what else we knew and fit it all to this setting.

Homer's face fell. "Well, you know, my villa has the actual desk where he wrote the James Bond novels. Most folks don't get to see that. It's the chance of a lifetime. Homer Johnson will make you feel right at home. There's lots of rooms. You could even stay a night."

"Uh, thanks, but—"

"I know a lot about spies too."

"You do?" asked Angel, now giving him a special smile. "How much?"

"I like to think it's more than almost anyone else knows. Yep, made it my life's passion. All of that secret-intelligence stuff, not only Bond."

"How about the Cuban Missile Crisis?" asked Angel.

"Of course."

"Stanley Shick?" asked Angel. She was good.

I watched for hesitation, for a swallow. But he just grinned. "My, don't you know your stuff, little lady. He's a rather obscure one, though many are. Code name Guy, eliminated in September of '62. The story is that he had some association with the missile crisis. Curious you'd put those things together." He eyed the two of us. "Very few people know about Shick. It was classified information until recently."

Half an hour later, we entered Ian Fleming's house at Goldeneye. It was, of course, even more awesome than our villa. It wasn't in the main part of the resort with all the other buildings but a five-minute walk away, over a bridge and in a private area on a hill, overlooking its own stunning white-sand private beach. It was a sprawling one-floor, white-stone, almost ranch-style house set on a very green lawn with lush tropical plants and flowers and a private pool. The interior of the house, even on this warm day, seemed air-conditioned by nature, with the breezes blowing gently through the open doors and windows.

It felt so cool inside—cool in every sense. It had inde-scribable style. Cool walls, cool floors, cool decoration—it was cool just to be here where he once was. It was like you were back in the best times of the 1960s.

There were pictures of Fleming everywhere, with other famous people. I imagined the parties that had taken place here! Angel was enthralled. I looked for Roald Dahl and Graham Greene or John Le Carré among the many black-and-white photographs but didn't see them. No shots of Grandpa either, not even lurking in the background. I searched for the name Stanley Shick or Guy Hicks but didn't see them either.

Then there was the desk, *the* desk, where Fleming had written every single James Bond novel. This was where he had created *him*. His novels actually weren't so great, but what a character, what an influence on popular culture! Was it a good influence? It was all about guns and beautiful women, expensive cars and martinis ("shaken, not stirred"), and a stud of a secret agent.

But as interesting as all of this was, Angel and I weren't there to be tourists. We just wanted to pick this weirdo's brain. That was foremost in my mind… until I saw several Walther PPKs sitting on a table with a couple other pistols and a stack of clips filled with bullets. There were three or four suppressors too. Everything was out in the open.

"Wow," I said, looking down at them. Angel and I exchanged a glance.

"Yes," said Johnson with pride. He picked up one of the pistols. It looked very old. "This is a Beretta 418, which was James Bond's first gun until an arms expert told Fleming that it was a 'lady's gun' with no real 'man-stopping ability.' So 007 stopped using it after *From Russia With Love*—the novel, I mean. They mostly employed PPKs in the movies, from Connery through Lazenby, Moore and Dalton, until Brosnan turned to a P99. But Craig has brought the PPK back, the classic."

He smiled and picked up the model that was exactly like Grandpa's, a black 7.65mm.

"Would you like to hold it?" he asked.

"Sure," I said.

He handed it to me. Every time I held one of these babies, it gave me a thrill…and also made me feel bad. I mean bad as in "not good." It fit right into your hand, so practical and deadly.

"Yes, James Bond's weapon of choice. Hitler's too, by the way."

I set it down.

He started showing us around the house. His pride and joy seemed to be the "007 bedroom," which was the master suite. He smiled at Angel as he showed it off, which was kind of creepy. I tried to turn his mind to other things.

"You must know all sorts of inside facts about the missile crisis."

"Well, the public doesn't know what really went on—never does. People think it was just Kennedy and Khrushchev in a showdown. You know, they always talk about JFK going on TV and telling the nation that we were on the brink of nuclear war and Khrushchev doing the same sort of thing back in the Soviet Union, firing off inflammatory letters about world destruction, but it involved many other players. There were secret things going on all the time, and by that I don't mean just the CIA's U2 spy planes flying over Cuba and taking pictures of the missiles being constructed."

"Spies?"

"Yeah, lots of them. The CIA knew all about their missiles and capabilities, and their spooks knew about ours. That takes a lot of boots on the ground."

"When things got hot in 1962," asked Angel, "what really happened behind the scenes?"

"Well, first of all, imagine that there are several hundred million lives at stake on both sides, and the fate of the world is hanging in the balance. You have dictators in the Soviet Union and Cuba freaking out, and Kennedy in the White House trying not to unleash his huge army or press a button to drop the nuclear bomb…and people from both sides in a secret meeting in a Chinese restaurant in suburban Washington."

"Really?" I said.

"But the real legwork was likely done by secret agents of ours inside the Soviet Union and those working for the bad guys inside the US of A. There were likely all sorts of very secret and dangerous get-togethers."

"Was Stanley Shick part of it?"

"I would bet he was, though no one can say for sure. He'd definitely be a candidate." Johnson walked over to his laptop, which he kept on a separate desk littered with notes. "I may have an image of him somewhere." He sat down. Angel and I quickly moved over and stood behind him, eyes locked on the screen.

"Ah, yes, there he is. This isn't very clear. There aren't many photos of him."

The image came onto the screen. It was grainy, so it was hard to make out the exact features of the man looking back at us. But I had seen many photos of my grandfather in his youth and middle age, and this wasn't him.

Why had Grandpa taken this man's place? I thought. Did he help to kill him?

"Shick was eliminated for sure?" I asked.

"Well, not for sure, my boy. Nothing is for sure in the world of espionage, but he vanished on the eve everything was going down across the water in Cuba. My theory is that he was sacrificed somehow. He knew something. Maybe one side wasted him, needed to. Maybe he was a double agent or maybe a double agent was the cause of his elimination. Maybe someone gave him up."

You are a traitor. The words on the envelope came back to me like a bullet to the heart. The other words too: *You deserve to die.* They now had an ominous meaning. I burned to know who wrote them, and what *W* meant. Did W pen those words…in anger?

"Ever heard of a spy named David McLean?" I asked.

"Donald, yes. Not David."

I remembered Angel mentioning that name back in Bermuda. "Could it be the same guy?" I asked, spelling out Grandpa's last name.

"Donald's last name began with *M-A-C*," said Homer. "He was one of the Cambridge Five double agents, pretty famous. Kim Philby and all, you know."

I felt some relief: saved by an extra *A*.

"But now that you mention it," mused Homer, "David McLean...that seems a little familiar. Can't place it though."

I didn't like the sound of that.

"Does the letter *W* mean anything to you in spy terms?"

He gave me a suspicious look. "Why would you ask that? Sounds like you know something. *W*?" To my relief, he grinned. "Maybe William Stephenson? Spy master!"

"We should go," I said. "Thanks for the tour."

On the way out I looked at the Walther PPK again, and the magazine clips with the bullets, and the suppressors. I remembered my desire to arm myself. I didn't want to, but I had no idea what we could be in for. Angel saw my look.

"Mr. Johnson," she said, gaining his attention. He glanced over at her. She pulled up her sweatshirt just enough to expose her stomach. "Something bit me right here, probably a local insect. You must know about them. You seem awfully well informed." She actually batted her eyes at him. She was full of surprises. "I hope it wasn't something poisonous. Care to take a look?"

His gaze locked onto her bare midriff. Mine did too, actually, for an instant. Her skin was smooth and beautiful, and her waist awfully slim and curvy under that old sweatshirt. It was very surprising, almost shocking. But I knew my job. I stepped back and palmed one of the suppressors and a clip of PPK bullets, six to the magazine.

SIXTEEN

SCENE ON THE BEACH

Back at our villa, I hid the bullets, the suppressor and the gun in a drawer, under my clothes. We had a lot to think about. But it was maddening how none of the information we'd gained, whether from our own work or from Leon's or from talking to that kook in the Ian Fleming Villa, seemed to be getting us any further. It was like a whole bunch of pieces to a puzzle that didn't fit together. We talked for a while and then Angel said she had to take a shower.

I started to pace.

W.

I knew the letter *W* was the key. But what did it mean? My mind went back to the Walther PPK. Maybe Grandpa had left it with his possessions as a sign. Maybe the gun was indeed the W.

I took the pistol out of the drawer and held it in my hand. Man, I couldn't get enough of it. It felt perfectly balanced. I felt like James Bond every time I gripped it. I struck a pose again, pointing it at the mirror, right hand extended, right leg slightly forward. I looked down at the gun, then took out the clip and snapped it into the butt. Wow, that felt cool! I pulled the slide back. It was cocked! I was locked and loaded. The gun was pitch black, just like Daniel Craig's, not much longer than my fully extended hand, with a dark black "beaver tail" butt, silver at the trigger and grayish black on the barrel, where I could read the name *Carl Walther* and some long German word that ended in *Waffen*, which I think meant "weapon." And right above the butt was a little symbol, kind of like a flag with a single word etched into it. *WALTHER*...with a *W*.

"Bond," I whispered to myself. "James Bond."

This was stupid. I was celebrating killing someone. I slumped down on the bed, took out my phone and googled *Take apart Walther PPK*. A YouTube video came up showing me how to do it.

What if the answer was inside the gun, the one I'd been carrying around ever since I pulled it out of Grandpa's possessions? I looked down at the screen and watched some NRA guy or whoever the heck he was going on about the fabulous PPK, almost salivating about it, as if a gun replaced God for him or something. Then I followed his instructions for taking the piece apart. But I already had it cocked, so first I had to remedy that. I dropped out the clip and its bullets, then fastened the suppressor to the end of the barrel. The silencer was just a round black steel tube. Cool. The pistol was twice its original length now, very James Bond. I pulled the trigger. The sound was just a loud *click*, but I imagined I had really fired. I saw the bullet exploding from the barrel. Wow, what a sensation! I tried to picture the bullet hitting something; then I stopped. *Bad Adam.* Guys like this stuff way too much. I was glad Angel was in the shower. I calmed myself and remembered my task. Now that the gun was uncocked, I took the silencer off the barrel. Then I put the safety on. I pulled the trigger guard down, just as the guy in the video had demonstrated, and then jerked the slide back until it came entirely off. The inside of the barrel was now exposed. I could see the innards of the weapon, the spring on the barrel: its brains, if not its soul. It was funny how benign it looked, like the inside of a simple little machine or even like one of the water pistols I used to have at home. But I could do so much more with this, cause so much damage. I could hurt people, take their lives.

I examined it closely and sighed. There wasn't a single thing inside it that helped me. No message from Grandpa, no little treasure, no *W* of any sort. It was just the inside of a Walther PPK, a mindless miniature killing machine. I snapped it back together and put it away in the drawer.

"Hey," said Angel behind me as I closed the drawer. I turned around. She looked exactly the same as before. How did she do that? She was still in her sweats and her hair still looked dry, almost greasy. Usually when you come out of a shower, you look transformed, or shouldn't you? And don't girls really look different? I know Shirley did.

"Hey," I said back. I really didn't want to talk just now, about anything. I was frustrated with the whole situation. I needed to take a break.

"I'm going swimming," I said. "Coming?"

She looked down. "No."

"That's not the correct answer."

"I...I don't feel like it."

I knew this had something to do with her being seen in a bathing suit. Man, I thought, Angel should be proud of herself, no matter what.

"Why not?"

"I just don't want to."

"What if I said that you are either coming swimming with me or you don't get a flight out of here? You're stuck." I'd never do that to her. It just came out of my mouth. It seemed to me that a real friend would push her about this. The easy thing was to just let her say no.

She didn't have enough money for a flight anywhere. She looked at me, gauging whether I was serious. She likely knew I wasn't. But it ticked her off anyway. I could see the anger rising in her face. She was turning red, and I thought she was going to hit me. She looked kind of cool, actually, when she was mad.

"All right," she said bitterly. "Let's go." She picked up her bag, violently pulled out her ugly one-piece bathing suit and stamped toward the bathroom.

As she did, she stumbled, of course, and caught the suit on the bedpost while trying to brace herself from the fall. She succeeded, but in her frustration, she yanked on the suit to get it free as if she wanted to destroy it. And that's what she did. It ripped from top to bottom. She'd almost torn it in half.

"Oh!" she said, her anger draining. "I guess I can't go after all."

"All right, I'll swim alone," I said.

I wondered if this amazing person, who had so much to offer, was going to miss out on a lot in life. I pulled my suit out of my bag and headed for the bathroom. She stood nearby with her arms crossed over her chest, her head down. She looked disappointed in herself. I felt bad. Someone needed to push her.

I turned back to her. "Why do you hide in those baggy clothes all the time?"

She sighed, her head still down.

"You don't need to be a bathing beauty, Angel. I'm not."

I could see her smile a little.

"Let's just go for a swim."

She looked up at me. There was always a bit of distrust in her eyes. There was always a bit of a front—Angel the tough girl who didn't need anyone, afraid that her real self wasn't good enough to be seen. I guessed it made sense, given her upbringing. But she looked at me now and dropped the façade. She had made a decision. "All right," she said quietly, "but what will I do for a suit?"

I smiled.

Ten minutes later, we were at the ritzy resort shop, which was full of tourist things but also clothes and bathing suits, everything for the beach. Problem was, they had no one-piece suits. All they had were trendy, expensive bikinis. And every last one of them was awfully skimpy.

I wondered what she would do. She marched over like someone steeling herself to take an "I-dare-you" dive off a steep rock and grabbed a white one with thin spaghetti straps on the top and a belt on the bottom. She went into the change room and tried it on, put her sweats back on over it and came out. "It's fine," she grunted. "I look ridiculous."

"I'll meet you at the beach," I said, then added, "It'll be fine." She looked away as I paid for the suit.

I went back to our room and put on my trunks. I wondered if she'd really do it, if she'd actually show up on the beach. I felt kind of guilty that I'd pushed her a bit. But I just wanted her to have some fun.

When I hit the beach, I couldn't see her anywhere. Then I looked out to the water and saw a head out there—just a head. But I could tell it was her, totally immersed in the water, probably standing on her tiptoes.

I motioned to her to come forward. She motioned for me to move toward her. I took a few steps, then beckoned for her to take a few too. She made a motion with her head like she was rolling her eyes. She moved forward, her neck and collarbones above the surface. I moved toward her again. Most of her face was usually hidden behind her hair. She'd left her shades on the beach and she'd had her head underwater, so her hair was slicked back, looking, actually, very cool, and showing her whole face for the first time. I almost took a step back. She looked different. I couldn't believe it was even her. Her fully exposed eyes were almond shaped, and her cheekbones high. I smiled at her and gave her a thumbs-up. That was when she truly started emerging from the water. It was also when I almost collapsed on the beach. She was moving steadily toward me, bashful, head partially down, blue eyes like the sea looking straight at me. The water fell from her shoulders and down her chest and along her slender waist to her hips and strong legs until she was fully visible in her racy white bikini.

Angel Dahl was…was stunning.

That was Bad Adam thinking. Or was it?

But wherever that thought came from, it was true.

Then…she tripped. But it didn't matter. When she raised herself up and smiled sheepishly at me, she looked even better.

I had been frozen on the spot on the sunny beach. But now I walked toward her (*staggered* might be a better word), and she came right up to me.

"Wow," was all I said, barely above my breath, but she heard it. I think my mouth was hanging open.

She tried to keep back her smile. "Don't tease," she said. "I look gross." With that she turned and ran into the waves, and I ran after her (what else could I do?), spraying water at her while she sprayed it back. We frolicked for a while, laughing and grabbing each other, throwing one another down into the blue blanket that was the warm Goldeneye water.

In the back of my mind, I kept wondering, Did Angel *really* think she was unattractive? Was she *that* modest and *that* worried about her looks that even her figure looked bad to her? Maybe some girls are like that—they have no idea how beautiful they are. Or did she know how spectacular she looked? Was she playing me? Was there more to learn about her, another side, maybe a darker Angel?

But being with her out there was so much fun that I stopped thinking about all that. We kept moving farther and farther out into the water, well beyond all the other swimmers. At one point, I picked her up and put her on my shoulders, somehow keeping both of us afloat. She felt light. As she screamed, I fired her into the air like a bullet out of a Walther PPK. She went headfirst into the waves in a spectacular crash. When she came up for air, her back to me, she was facing the shoreline out past the Goldeneye beach, well beyond the swimming area. The resort's guests weren't supposed to go there.

"*W!*" she suddenly cried out.

"What?"

"*W!*" She was pointing toward the out-of-bounds shore. "Look!"

There was water in my face. I swept it off and squinted into the distance.

I couldn't believe it. Over on the shoreline in the direction she pointed I saw the clear shape of a *W* in the rocks!

SEVENTEEN

W?

The W was distinct. Though it was part of a natural rock formation, it almost looked like someone had placed the big letter there, like God had reached his hand down and set the letter on the shoreline.

"Am I making too much of it?" Angel asked, treading water, trying to contain her excitement. "Am I seeing things?"

I didn't answer. I just started power-swimming toward it. I'm a pretty good swimmer (my size helps), yet Angel stayed right with me. She was as sleek and fit as a dolphin, gliding fast through the water. I had the feeling that this girl was keeping herself in shape in a big way. Anxious to be accepted, highly critical of herself and a terrible judge of her own worth, she had unknowingly made herself into something remarkable.

It didn't take us long to get there.

W marked the spot, I kept thinking. It sounded like a line a pirate might say. What will we find when we get there, I wondered, a hidden treasure of some sort?

The W actually formed the opening of a crevice in the rocky shoreline, which was about six or seven feet high here. We pulled ourselves up onto the rocks and went inside. The walls looked the same all over—craggy and rocky. Was there something inside one of the cracks in the walls? We started searching. We searched for a long time. We didn't really know exactly what we were looking for—though I had the feeling that if I saw it, I would recognize it instantly. But the rocks were so uniform that nothing stood out, the cracks were only inches deep and empty, and the surface was so hard that you couldn't pry any of it off or break into it to see what was in or behind it. Before long, the sun was getting low in the Caribbean sky. It was no use. We'd have to come back with lights.

We returned to Goldeneye, swimming on our backs, looking at the W and the crevice behind it as we moved away. As we got farther from it, the whole thing became dim and then went out of sight. I began to wonder. Had it really looked like a *W* or had we imagined it? We couldn't afford to be wrong. By late tomorrow morning we *had* to leave Goldeneye. We couldn't even try to stay here secretly after check-out time. There was just too much security. We'd never get away with it, and any attempt might land us in serious trouble.

The Walther PPK wasn't the W, this rock formation might be a dead end too, and how could William Stephenson possibly be what or who we were looking for? He was long gone from earth, and I had no tangible evidence to connect him in any way to my grandfather.

I had to look somewhere else for W. But now I was down to my last few hours.

We stayed on our backs the entire distance to the beach. It was a relaxing way to swim, and I needed to try to be calm because I was starting to freak out. My mission had utterly failed. I had spent nearly all the money and only discovered that my grandfather was a horrible human being who had tried to kill me. What would I tell the other guys? Could I harbor such a secret about Grandpa from Mom, from everyone, for the rest of my life? It was mission unaccomplished.

Then it got worse.

As we reached shallow water, we stood up, gave one last look out across the surface toward the now-vanished W and turned toward the beach.

"Good evening, you two," said a voice. I recognized the smooth Bermudian tone.

John.

EIGHTEEN

VILLAIN

"Had enough play time?" he asked.

"Hi, John," said Angel, trying to sound normal and cheery, as if the two of us had simply decided to come to Goldeneye for some vacation time.

"Looking for something out there?"

It was time to lay our cards on the table. He kind of had us anyway. And we were getting nowhere on our own. I needed to involve John, even if he was the enemy. Maybe he'd say something incriminating.

"W," I said.

He laughed as if he was relieved.

"I have to tell you, Mr. Murphy, I have no idea what that is all about. Why do you keep saying that? What does the letter *W* have to do with anything? You've seen too many James Bond movies. Ah, the secret clue, the secret letter! I will be totally honest with you. The letter *W* plays absolutely no role in any of this. Honestly."

He was poker-faced. He didn't swallow or blink. It was almost too good. What if he wasn't lying? What if W indeed meant nothing? But it had been on the gate, on the envelope, and, most importantly, Grandpa had said it over and over to himself in the mirror when he didn't know that Angel was listening. I told John all three of those things, laid out the case for W.

"First of all, he knew you were listening to him, Angel."

"He did?"

"Yeah. He's more skilled than you will ever be." Yes, I thought, but he underestimates her. We all do.

John went on, "Mr. Know is a strange man, very eccentric, but he doesn't mean you harm."

I thought I caught the telltale swallowing, but he went on quickly.

"I told you before, I'm one of the good guys—or at least I'm on their side."

"So you aren't going to kill us?" asked Angel.

He laughed. "No." His face turned more serious. "But I am going to watch you. If you don't go home now, you could indeed be in danger. You shouldn't be here. You told me you weren't coming. You both lied."

I thought of Huckleberry Finn. John was lying too, about something. I was sure of it.

"I understand that you are leaving tomorrow. That's a good thing. I will watch you and then escort you out of here. This time, Adam, you will go home and not come back." He turned to Angel. "As will you, my dear."

"I'm not your dear!"

"We found something," I said.

When he turned back to me, his mouth had become a straight line. "What?" he asked.

"Out there." I pointed out toward the water. "Marked by a *W*."

"Out where?" he said. I could see his hand moving toward his gun holster.

"On the shoreline, just outside the resort property."

His face broke into a grin, and his hand moved away from his gun. "On the shoreline? A massive *W*, was it? What, are you pirates looking for hidden treasure now?" He laughed out loud.

"I've got to get changed," said Angel and began marching toward our villa. John, to my surprise, let her go.

"My, my, Angel," he said, "you are certainly all grown up." He was eyeing her up and down as she walked away. I wanted to slug him. I caught up to her and took her hand. John followed us.

"Creep," said Angel under her breath.

At the villa, he started issuing orders, telling us to stay indoors that night and be prepared to meet him at noon where the shuttles gathered so he could accompany us to the airport. Then he asked to see the envelope. I supposed it couldn't do any harm, so I let him have it. He sat at the desk and examined it for a while, holding it up to the strong light of the lamp, chuckling at the words on it saying that my grandfather was a traitor and that he deserved to die. Then he started looking at the *W*. He examined it for the longest time. Then he grinned.

"Come here," he finally barked at me. He pointed at the envelope. "That's not just a *W*. If you look very, very carefully, you'll see there is an *h* right beside it, barely perceptible. It's the beginning of a word. How many words start with *Wh* in the English language, my boy? Quite a few, and very common ones, wouldn't you say? You were simply looking at the first two letters of another word, not a *W*!"

I examined it closely. I could see the *h* now, barely visible but there. He was right! That letter on the envelope was not a standalone *W*. I had just *wanted* to see it that way to make things fit. Maybe we'd been on the wrong trail all along.

After John left, Angel said, "He's up to something, something bad."

"There weren't people in Jamaica waiting for us, were there?" I said. "He lied about that. That was a real stretcher."

"A what?"

"Nothing. But he's hiding something, you're right."

"And maybe we need to find out what that is?"

"I have the feeling that we shouldn't get on the shuttle with John tomorrow. I don't think it would be good for our health."

I looked out a window. It was dark outside, though a bright moon illuminated the beach.

"I don't think he's watching us at all."

"Do you think he might come back when we are asleep and…?" She didn't want to finish the sentence.

"Let's get out of here."

"But where should we go?"

"Let's stay with Ian Fleming tonight."

Ten minutes later, Homer Johnson was greeting us at his door. It was loud inside.

"Hello, Leon and Shirley!" he cried, a martini in his hand. It was probably "shaken, not stirred." He sounded a little tipsy. "Have you come for the party?"

"We'd like to take you up on your offer and stay the night, if that's okay," said Angel. The Goldeneye brochure had said that Ian Fleming Villa could accommodate eight.

"Ah, getting that James Bond vibe, are you? Of course—the more the merrier." He opened the door wide and we could see that a party was in full swing, though lots of the partygoers looked old and very unhip—lots of ugly shorts and flowery shirts, lots of ponytails…on the men. They were playing sixties music, though not the Beatles or the Stones. It was early-sixties stuff, Shirley Bassey at first and later on, Burt Bacharach, which I recognized as something my grandfather used to play, kind of jazzy and apparently cool in its day.

We stepped inside.

"I'll give you the 007 suite," he said, winking at us. The music was so loud that he had to shout.

Angel didn't bat an eye. She thanked him, said we were tired and took my hand and led me to the bedroom. Bad Adam was getting pretty excited. I was frantically thinking about Shirley.

The 007 suite was a big room with a low bed and lots of pillows. I immediately took them and laid them out on the floor, so I'd have a place to sleep. *You idiot,* said Bad Adam.

"You're the idiot," I responded.

"Pardon me?" asked Angel. She looked a little shocked.

I'd said it out loud! "Nothing!" I said quickly. "Uh, sometimes I talk to myself, say strange things, that's all. I have a side of me that asks me to do stupid things. I have to fend him off."

"Bad Adam?"

I almost fell to the floor.

"What?" I asked.

"I have this side of me that I call Bad Angel. It's a pretty big side, but it's not really me. I have to fight her off too."

I couldn't believe it. We were a perfect match.

"That's weird," I said and tried to laugh it off. Inside, I was trying very hard to think of Shirley.

Angel got into bed, clothes on. I got down on the floor on the pillows, clothes on.

Half an hour later I was wide awake, and I knew she was too.

"Angel?"

"Yes?" she answered quickly.

Something had dawned on me.

"We need to get out of here. When I told John that we found something *out there*, he was pretty upset. He only calmed down when I said exactly where we looked. I think John has something to do tonight *out there* somewhere—something sinister. That's why he was cautioning us to not come to Goldeneye; that's why he told us to stay inside tonight."

"Which means we need to go outside."

"Exactly. Whatever he came here to do, I want to know what it is."

We got up and slipped out of the suite. Because Homer had given us the tour earlier, we knew there was a back entrance. We sneaked to it, our exit covered by the noise of the swinging sixties sounds. In the vestibule at the back door was a bunch of black wet suits and scuba-diving equipment. We both seemed to get the same idea at once.

The black wet suits would perfectly camouflage us in the night. We could sneak around better with them on. The scuba tanks and masks might come in handy too. Maybe we could swim out to the *W* again and get a closer look at things with no one nearby.

Moments later we were on the beach in the wet suits, carrying the scuba-diving equipment. The suits were skintight, and I couldn't believe how great Angel looked in hers. Or at least Bad Adam couldn't. But that wasn't what intrigued me the most as I walked beside her onto the Goldeneye beach. Someone was standing at the far end of it. He was dropping his possessions against the short stone wall that ringed the area as he pulled on a wet suit and scuba tanks. We could see him in the bright moonlight.

It was John.

We ducked down behind a small table and umbrella.

He stood up and looked around. Then he headed into the water.

We followed. Angel had told me she knew how to dive, and I had dived before (I'd had my maiden scuba adventure just a few months earlier, with Mom and Dad in southern Florida), so we had no trouble keeping up. The problem was, we had to stay fairly close to him. We could see for some distance in the moonlight, but not very far.

We moved along, terrified that he might turn around and spot us at any moment. We'd carried our bags with us and dropped them on the beach, not far from John's things but out of the way, so he couldn't spot them in the dark. The gun was back there too. I had put Homer Johnson's bullet clip in it, six bullets, ready for action. I'd even attached the silencer. It wouldn't do me any good underwater.

As we swam I worried about what I'd do if he turned and attacked me and, more important, how I'd protect Angel. I had to look after her.

We kept moving, a long distance. I started worrying that he had some sort of underwater weapon, perhaps a mini-harpoon or something. He might suddenly kill us. Maybe he was drawing us far out into the water on purpose. A spy would do something like that. It would be perfect. He could murder us and we would just disappear. If anyone noticed our stuff on the beach, they'd assume we'd drowned on a late-night romantic swim, perhaps alcohol fueled. Bleeding far from shore, we'd be food for sharks.

Ominous music—bass and drums—played in my mind as we followed him. I prayed that he wouldn't turn around.

We trailed him for ten minutes or so. The water got very deep. Then he dove down and looked around, as if searching for something. After a while he found what looked like an odd pile of stones and began to pull them away, one by one. Then he took out a mini-shovel he had on his belt and began to dig. We kept our distance. Suddenly, he dropped the shovel and pumped his fist in a slow underwater motion. Then he reached down and pulled something out of the hole he had dug. He looked around, jammed the shovel into the seafloor and turned toward us!

We got out of sight as quickly as we could behind a rock formation and made sure we were behind him as he headed back toward the shore. He didn't seem to spot us. Whatever he was carrying was heavy, and it appeared to take a great deal of effort for him to swim. We all moved slowly in the direction of the beach. He emerged onto the sand and we stayed in shallow water, our eyes barely above the surface, watching him. He was lugging something along the beach, but we couldn't see exactly what he was doing or what was in his hands. I needed to know. I couldn't shake the feeling that if I could see what he had, everything in this mystery would become clear. The moment had arrived. I crouched up out of the water and moved onto the beach, Angel behind me, holding my hand. She was shaking. I squeezed her hand to comfort her and looked around to reassure her.

When I turned back, John was staring at us. He had dropped whatever he had, reached down and pulled something out of his bag. It was a gun. And it wasn't a Walther PPK. This pistol was bigger and more modern. In fact, it looked really big. I soon realized he had a silencer on it. I knew he could easily pick us off, even in the moonlight and from fifty feet away.

He could do it fairly quietly. There was no one around. He motioned for us to come forward. I held Angel's hand tighter. She was really shaking now. He had us and didn't look pleased. *This was for real.* As we approached, I could see what he had dropped to the sand. Two bars of gold!

He kept motioning to us until we were just seven or eight feet away, side by side. He looked even more intense up close, more serious. He meant business. He cocked the gun. I heard Angel give out a little cry. I had to do something.

"If you are going to shoot us anyway," I said, "then tell me this. Is that old man back there in Bermuda really my grandfather? He must be. He even wears his cologne."

John hesitated. "I...I can't. I actually would like to, but I can't." It was a bizarre answer. "But I'll tell you this. Mr. Know was used at the most delicate moments in the Cuban Missile Crisis."

"Used?" I said.

He looked like he had said too much or at least hadn't expressed himself as he wished. "I'll tell you something else." He looked a little angry. "Your grandfather, Mr. Know, was a traitor."

My heart sank. "So it is him!"

"I didn't say that—not exactly. But he was a traitor. Although sometimes you have to do what you have to do." That sounded like a sentence DJ had read from Grandpa's journal back at the cottage. I wished my big cousin was here at this very moment. I needed him.

John pointed the gun at Angel's head.

Instinctively, I stepped in front of her. "Run," I whispered.

But she didn't move. It was as if she was frozen to the spot, mesmerized. "You'd do this for me?" I heard her say under her breath, almost crying, speaking half to me, half to herself. It wasn't a cry of fear. It was the cry of someone who had been left on a doorstep as a baby, someone who hadn't been wanted, who had been unloved, someone for whom no one had ever made a sacrifice. Good Adam had acted. Bad Adam was dying.

Then Angel stepped out from behind me. Like lightning, John pointed the gun at her. But even faster than that, Angel hit the ground, rolled toward John and scissor-kicked his legs out from under him. He hit the sand with a thump. Was that a "silent killing" move? My backpack was only ten feet or so away, behind a bush. I darted toward it. The loaded Walther PPK was just inside, on top. I opened the bag in an instant and turned toward John, cocking the gun as I did. I was locked and loaded and in my James Bond pose, silencer on, barrel pointed toward him, right hand extended, right foot pointing toward my target.

Instead of fleeing once she'd dropped John, Angel had actually come at him again. She had other moves. Bad Adam wasn't laughing at her claims anymore. She grabbed John by the arm, the one that held the gun. She looked like she was trying to bend it back, to lock him into a submission hold.

But John was John for good reason. He moved so fast that I couldn't even tell what he did. Then somehow Angel was on the ground, hitting it hard, and John had trained his gun on her head, two feet away.

That's when I shot him.

I couldn't believe it when I did it. It was just a response, a reaction. I nailed him right in the chest. There was the slight jolt of the bullet leaving my legendary pistol, the hiss of it sucking through the air and the *THWACK* of it striking him in the middle of his body, heart area, dead on target. *Man down!* Bad Adam felt exhilaration course through his body like a jolt of electricity. *Wow!* Bad Adam had saved the girl and terminated the bad guy! It was a video-game triumph come to life!

But I didn't feel triumphant. I felt horrible. I had killed a human being. I didn't care how bad he was. I didn't even care what he had been about to do. He lay there on the ground, not moving at all.

Angel was silent. She looked at me in disbelief. "You shot him!" she said. She didn't seem pleased, didn't seem happy the way a girl would be in the movies. I wasn't her hero at that moment, and I didn't feel that way anyway. I didn't want to walk away now, with the bikini-clad babe wrapped in my arms, to the sound of cool music. I just wanted to hang my head.

She dropped down and put her fingers to John's throat.

"He's alive!" she whispered. Then she felt his chest, her fingers on the spot where the bullet had hit him. Even in the moonlight, we could see that there wasn't any blood. Then she felt the rest of his chest.

"He's wearing a bulletproof vest!" Even underwater, even here, John had come prepared. He was clearly an experienced spy.

I breathed a sigh of relief, and so did Angel.

"You stopped him," she said and leaped up and hugged me. That felt pretty good. In fact, it felt great. I didn't even have time to think of Shirley. But I also realized, even in that happy moment, that John had simply been knocked down, perhaps hitting his head as he fell, and was temporarily stunned. He might get up at any moment. In fact, we now heard him groan. Knowing John was always well prepared for any eventuality, I ripped through his backpack and found a pair of handcuffs. I pulled his hands behind his back and snapped them on. As I did that, Angel found a small coil of rope in his bag and tied his feet together. It was a pretty good knot. This was some kind of girl!

John groaned more and started coming around.

"So you were after gold," I said to him, glancing down at the two bars. "I'll assume there's more of it out there." I picked up one of them. It was heavy. I noticed some lettering on the side and the stamp of a foreign bank: Russian letters.

"What's the deal, John?" asked Angel.

He wouldn't say a word.

I started looking through his bag, digging down deep into it. There were knives, more rope, extra clothes, a cell phone, but nothing to tell me what I really wanted to know.

"*W marked the spot.* What does that mean, John?"

He said nothing. I remembered him saying that he knew nothing about the letter *W*, and he had seemed to mean it.

"What is W?" Angel asked him, louder. "Or who is he?"

The second she said that, it came to me like a shot from a PPK.

"It's two words!" I told her.

"What?"

"Double You."

NINETEEN

DOUBLE YOU

"Double You marked the spot," said Angel, amazed.

"All you heard back in Bermuda, when you secretly listened to Mr. Know, was him saying the *sound* double you. It wasn't a *letter*. He was saying two words. And when he said it, he was looking at himself in the mirror."

"You're way off," grunted John.

"I think the lady doth protest too much," I said.

Angel laughed out loud. John looked perplexed.

I glanced down into his bag, reached in and picked up his cell phone.

"Don't touch that!" cried John.

"Shut up!" said Angel.

I checked his list of contacts. One was Know. I sent out my call, across the waves toward Bermuda.

"Hello?" an old voice said. I'd forgotten that my grandfather was over ninety. He always seemed so much younger. But that one word—*Hello*—didn't sound like him, didn't even sound the way his voice had back there in his office in Bermuda when he sentenced me to death.

"This is Adam McLean Murphy."

There was a long pause. I imagined him swallowing.

"Yes, Adam. It is so good to hear from you." He sounded just like my beloved grandfather again. "Come back to Bermuda. I'll explain everything. I wasn't trying to kill you. I would have saved you at the last moment. I was testing you. It's complicated. I'll explain."

"I'm sure you can," I said. Then I played my card. It was a bit of a stretcher, but sometimes that's what you have to do. "We have your boy John here, and he's explained everything," I said without emotion, turning my back on our captive so any sound he made couldn't be heard at the other end of the phone.

"I doubt that."

He'd played his card well too. John grinned up at me, noting that I'd paused, knowing that his boss was a tough nut to crack. I had to try a different approach. I wasn't even going to bother telling him that we had caught John red-handed with two bricks of vintage Soviet Union gold.

"Grandpa," I said, "why did you do that to me, even for a moment? I was very scared."

"I'm sorry, Adam. Come back here and I'll make things right."

I tried to sound sad. "When I was little, you always comforted me when I was upset."

"Yes."

"I often think about how you read to me to help me sleep. I always remember the line you emphasized in one of the stories. It went: *It is only with the heart that one can see rightly. What is essential is invisible to the eye.* Remember that?"

"Of course."

"It was from a Roald Dahl book, but I can't recall which one. Can you?"

There was a hesitation on the other end of the line, as if he had swallowed.

"No," he said.

I had him.

"It's not from Roald Dahl, you pig," I said. "It's from *The Little Prince* by Antoine de Saint-Exupéry, your *favorite* book. Let me correct that: my *grandfather's* favorite book!"

There was another pause, probably a couple of swallows.

"I...I'd forgotten that."

"No, you hadn't."

"Yes, I—"

"No, you hadn't." I let it sink in. "What's the deal, Stanley?"

There was an even longer pause. When the voice came back on the phone, it sounded nothing like Grandpa's.

"Dave McLean was a traitor!" he shouted.

"Like you?" I asked. "Like John here? You wrote that letter, didn't you? The one that said he deserved to die!"

"He did!"

"Why?"

There was another long pause. Even a secret agent, even a double agent, knows when he is cornered.

Stanley Shick, code name Guy Hicks, had nothing to gain anymore. The truth, as obscure as it was in this case, as obscure as it often is, had to come out.

"I'll tell you, you snotty punk, " he snarled. "He betrayed me!" He sounded like a madman, which was likely close to the truth.

"Yes, I was a double agent. But many were. I had to gain something in life. Both sides were bad anyway."

"That's a convenient way to look at it. Got some gold for yourself, did you?"

"The Soviets paid me for information. Fleming often had us down to his place in Jamaica, so I hid my stash at Goldeneye one night, way out in the water where no one could find it. I planned to come back and get it someday. But in the spring of 1962, they caught me. Your grandfather played a big role; typical of him to turn on his friends. We *were* friends."

"But you betrayed your country. Grandpa wouldn't have liked that."

"He betrayed me!" he shouted into the phone. *Madman.* "And then he did even worse."

"Worse?"

"Listen to this and imagine the depravity. Stephenson, that fool, had his hand on everything.

He was behind my capture, he and McLean. They had me under house arrest in Bermuda. I was scheduled to be tried secretly and executed. Bill would have made that happen fast. He could make anything happen. He was Canadian; he had his own rules."

I smiled a big smile at my end of the phone. I was thinking of my six amazing cousins from the Great White North.

"That was long before the missile crisis broke out, months before. But Stephenson knew what was going on in Cuba. He knew everything. He knew the missiles were there even before the U2 spy planes photographed them for the CIA. He knew it would all hit the fan soon. McLean was negotiating with the Soviets about it behind the scenes. Stephenson hadn't even told the president that McLean was kicking tires for him. He used the code name Adam."

I felt a lump in my throat.

"But then what McLean was doing got really dangerous. We had word through a double agent that the next time Dave came to Moscow he was going to meet with an unfortunate accident. It was a lead-pipe cinch. But the meeting had to happen. It was vital. Stephenson knew he had to send McLean in, send him to his death. So, in order to save his skin, they made me a proposition, the useless excuses for human beings!"

Madman.

"They offered me a deal. I was the same size as your grandfather. We had the same color eyes and hair, same build. We used to tease each other about being brothers from another mother…in the old days."

He actually sounded sad for a second.

"Stephenson came to me and said that if I took on a very dangerous mission inside the Soviet Union, they'd let me live. I would have to spend the rest of my life in Bermuda, under house arrest. But they'd let me have what I wanted there. They even, later, let me have the girl as my ward. I thought I might use her somehow to get away. But it never worked out."

I didn't say a word to Angel.

"But there was a catch, of course. I had to undergo plastic surgery, make my face look exactly like McLean's ugly mug. The instant I was healed enough, they'd insert me into the Soviet Union so I could undertake the very secret meetings in place of your grandfather. They told me they were doing this because it was awfully dangerous. BUT THEY DIDN'T SAY IT WAS LETHAL!!"

Madman.

"They were setting me up for death. It was an execution, an elimination, orchestrated by Stephenson and your beloved grandfather! I had zero chance of survival. But I didn't know that, and I had no choice anyway. I was to do this, undergo the painful surgery and live with looking like someone else for the rest of my life and be allowed to live, or simply be executed for my past crimes (as they saw them). So, I did it. And I survived!"

He sounded triumphant.

"I fooled them all! Oh, the commie thugs came for me, all right. Six of them on a dark rainy night in an alley in Moscow. *That's* what your grandfather knew would happen! And they smashed me up pretty badly, left me for dead. But I lived! I remember the look on Stephenson's face when I got home, after they'd gotten me out."

"They got you out? But—"

"With my lifelong injuries, my crippled face, my incarceration in Bermuda and my gold far away where I couldn't get my hands on it!"

"I saw your jail, Stanley. It didn't seem too shabby."

"I couldn't leave. Stephenson always kept two goons on me. Even after he died, he left them with me, in perpetuity, until the day I die! I was surprised they let me have the girl, but they watched out for her, kept her safe, I suppose, though I wouldn't have harmed her."

"But then there was John."

"I tried to get one of them to switch sides, but I never succeeded until John. I had been softening him up for a while. Then you came along. Oh, when I heard you were at my very doorstep…Dave McLean's grandson! You can't imagine how that felt! I had followed McLean on the Internet, knew what he was up to, about his daughters, his grandsons, even his death—which didn't cheer me up too much, since I wasn't the cause of it. All I'd been able to do over the years was get one single letter off to him. I didn't even know that he received it."

"He did. He kept it. He was a decent man. Maybe he felt badly, even though you were a traitor to your country."

"HE'S THE TRAITOR! I used to stand at the mirror at night and imagine killing him. I used to say out loud what I had become, what I hated. He was in that mirror looking back at me. I wanted to murder him. I said who I was, that despised thing."

"Double You."

That's what he calls himself now, I thought. It's like a code name. *Double You marked the spot*!

"Yes. But then you came to my very door, dropped right into my lap! I had the boys keep you outside for a while, while I did myself up, made myself look *exactly* like McLean. I remembered his voice—aged it a bit. I couldn't get at him, couldn't get my revenge, but out of the blue, I could kill his very grandson! Not only that, I could do it and make you think that he had done it to you! I remember the fear in your eyes! I remember the disbelief! You would die thinking that he had murdered you! You even looked like him! WHAT REVENGE!"

Madman.

"I got John and Jim to go along with the first part, not saying, of course, that I intended to actually eliminate you. But then I told John the truth, just him. I asked him into my office right before you were brought in and gave him the whole plan. I felt he was ready. I told him about the gold and where it was at Goldeneye. I told him that if he helped me, he could have it! ALL of it! I just wanted my revenge. I knew he'd do it for the gold. Jim didn't know that the Dahl building was rigged. It was something I'd done on the sly over the years. I don't know why; maybe I thought I could catch one of them in it and get away. I was, in my day, a mechanical genius. They thought I was just making repairs, being nostalgic about the time when Dahl was there. We told Jim that I was just testing you about something and we'd let you out after midnight. John was going to dispose of what was left of your body so there would be no trace of you by morning. But you got out! That bloody girl helped you! I never should have kept her! It was a soft moment."

Madman.

"And now everything has fallen apart. My revenge is lost!" He sounded like he was in tears. "But at least I've told you the ugly truth. At least I've told you in person what a useless, traitorous human being your grandfather was. You can take that to your grave!"

I didn't feel that way at all. Sure, my grandfather had told some stretchers. But he had to. Maybe sometimes you really had to, when it mattered, when a greater good was at stake. He and Stephenson had put this double agent out of service and the world was saved from destruction.

"They gave you a chance, Stanley," I said. "You were the traitor, and they still gave you your life. But you paid a price for your evil."

He was trying to respond when I hit the End button.

Angel and I looked at each other. The last thing I'd said had explained a great deal to her.

"He was just Stanley Shick, wasn't he? Not your grandfather."

I nodded. I'd give her the details later.

It seemed like it was over; we had learned the truth. But what were we going to do now? How could we explain John and these gold bricks and all these state secrets to the Goldeneye security or the Jamaican police? I'd fired a gun and tried to kill a man.

"I'll take care of all this," said a voice we didn't recognize. It came out of the darkness, and its owner was plodding toward us wearing sandals and a *Skyfall* T-shirt over his big belly and under his colorful beach shirt. The accent was British. He didn't sound tipsy at all now. It was Homer Johnson.

We were both gaping at him, so he kept talking.

"John has been identified as a risk for some time. We were watching him, watching out for Angel's safety for many years, actually. I followed you two from Bermuda to New York to Times Square, then you, Adam, to Chicago and here to Goldeneye. I'll clean up all this. I'll take the PPK too, thank you very much."

"But how did you follow us without—?"

"Assume the color of the wall and look like me. That's the secret." He grinned and then stuck out his hand for us to shake. "Bob Smith, MI6."

"Bob Smith?" said Angel. "Really?"

"No, not really, but it will do."

"But what do you actually look like?" I asked.

"Excuse me?"

"In real life, like when you are walking around in London, talking to MI6? Nice suits? How do you get that fat look?"

"I'm sorry," he said, "I don't follow you."

TWENTY

DENOUEMENT

We flew partway home together. Angel was told that Stanley Shick would not be in her home when she got there. They would remove him, just the way John had been removed to a holding cell in Miami. It was her home now. They told her the deed would be signed over into her name. There would also be extensive funds available to her: the money that had been set aside to house Shick. She could do as she pleased. She could go to the college of her choice.

It was New Year's Eve day when we reached New York. The airport was jammed with people. Everyone seemed to be in a good mood.

But Angel wasn't very happy, despite all the great news she had just gotten from Bermuda. She knew I was leaving her, going back to Shirley. And, of course, I was. It was the right thing to do, the good thing. She tried to kiss me at JFK, but that wouldn't have been fair to Shirley, so I stepped back. She wasn't having any of that—she darted toward me and gave me a hug and wouldn't let go. It was like she was going to hang on to me forever. She was wearing her sweats again.

"You know, Angel, a couple of times over the last few days I thought you were a double agent or something," I said, trying to break the mood. She was still holding on to me.

She stepped back and looked right at me. "What do you mean?"

"Well, throughout most of this I was worried that you weren't who you said you were, that you were working for the other side."

She kept looking up at me. "No," she said. "I'm just me." Her eyes were red. She paused, and when she spoke again, her voice was trembling. "Thank you for everything, Adam. Thank you for liking me for who I am and accepting me." She dropped her head and turned and walked away. I thought she mumbled something else. It sounded like "Because I like you." But I wasn't sure.

I had been really concerned that I would be choked up when I said goodbye to her, so I'd written her a note, which I'd secretly stuffed into her backpack. I thought of her reading it on the plane or in her room in Bermuda. It said:

May the rest of your life be as fabulous as these last few days were for me. You are the best, Angel. Don't let anyone ever tell you differently. You're a star. Have a great life.

I got onto the plane to Buffalo, feeling bad. But not just for her; for me too.

Up in the skies, I willed the plane forward. I remembered that Mom's flight was to come in at 2:00 PM and mine was scheduled to land at 1:45. I had told her that I'd be back from the cottage up north by last night. She had no idea I'd been in Bermuda,

New York City and Jamaica. In fact, when I thought about it, the last few days seemed like a dream, like a movie. I kept my backpack with me as carry-on luggage and rushed through the gates and out into the concourse. I glanced up at Mom's flight arrival time. It was early! And there she was!

I could see her approaching the baggage area. I turned around quickly, hoping she hadn't seen me, and rushed outside to grab a cab. I jumped in and asked the driver to get me home to Delaware Park on the fly. I told him I'd add a big tip. So we roared around the Thruway—that's the I-90, the highway that encircles the city—and headed home. I got there before Mom, raced up the front steps and opened the door. There was a note in the mail slot. I tore it out and rushed into my room. I loved our home. It wasn't just because we had such a great family—it was also because Shirley, my stupendous, beautiful, loving girlfriend, was there so often. I could hardly wait to see her!

My phone rang. It was a text from Mom.

Just got in. I'm stopping for a chai latte at Starbucks. We had a great time. You won't believe what we got up to. It will amaze you!

I smiled. I wasn't sure I would ever tell her what I'd been up to. She didn't need to know. It would only cloud her perception of Grandpa. He hadn't been an angel. He had done what was right—what, as he said, he needed to do. I was proud of him. I always would be.

Angel. I thought of her again. I looked down at the note. It was from Shirley. She was coming over for the New Year's Eve party tonight! My heart pounded as I thought of holding my girlfriend in my arms.

Then an image of Angel emerging from the water at Goldeneye came into my mind. She was such an incredible surprise. The way she looked had blown me away. I started thinking that Bad Adam was responsible for this coming back to me, but then I thought he wasn't. That was stupid thinking, excuses. There was no Bad Adam, really. There was just me. I had some bad impulses and some good ones, and I had to make up my mind which would govern me. I thought of Angel in the bikini again. She was so beautiful! And it was okay to think that, because she was. But more important, much more important, she was an amazing person.

"Whoa!" I said out loud to myself. "Forget her! Angel is gone."

I opened the message from Shirley. She often sent me love notes. I never show them to anyone. I smelled it. She usually perfumes them with her scent, which is *Radical Obsession* or something. All I know is I love it.

But this note had no scent.

It read:

Dear Adam,

I am sorry to tell you that I won't be coming to the party tonight at your house. I wish I had some pressing reason why I can't, but I have to be honest with you: I've met someone else. I actually started seeing him a few weeks ago, but I haven't been able to talk to you about it until now. I couldn't bring myself to speak to you face to face. I'm interested in someone else, Adam.

It wasn't you. It was me.

All the best to you, forever,

Shirley

I dropped the letter on the floor. It was as if someone had just died, someone desperately important. I had to go over to her house, talk to her! But I felt frozen. I fell back on the bed. She had said "forever," but she didn't mean it. She was with another guy! Some people are on your side forever, and others just aren't. I had known, deep down inside me, back in Bermuda when that man with Grandpa's face had turned against me, that it wasn't really him. My brain may not have realized it, but my soul knew. He would never betray me. He never will. *But Shirley, my Shirley…was a double agent.* She had given her allegiance to someone else.

I don't cry. I'm a guy. Or at least I don't do it in public or in front of my best friends or my girlfriend or my mom or dad or any living human being other than me. I readied myself for a waterfall now. Strangely, it didn't come. I didn't feel like shedding a single tear. I stood up. I actually felt okay. And I knew why.

I thought of someone who I was certain was on my side. I thought of the cell phone I had bought for that someone back in New York. I thought of a life of excitement stretching out in front of me.

Later that night, just before the stroke of midnight on New Year's Eve, I called Angel Dahl.

ACKNOWLEDGMENTS

Thanks, of course, go to all the good folks at Orca Book Publishers—editor Sarah Harvey, for her own bravery in dealing with me and my six other not-so-secret agents, to the intrepid boss Andrew Wooldridge and to co-conspirators Dayle Sutherland and Leslie Bootle. Thanks must also go to a chap named Ian Fleming and his great creation, James Bond, as well as to John Le Carré and what I learned from his creation, George Smiley, as he sneaked his way through *The Spy Who Came in from the Cold* and *Tinker Tailor Soldier Spy*. And not to be forgotten are Norah McClintock and those scoundrels Eric Walters, Sigmund Brouwer, Richard Scrimger, Ted Staunton and John Wilson, who make up the gang of Seven. It has been a pleasure to work with them both on paper and stage. Eric's Bermuda-based novel *Camp X: Trouble in Paradise* was helpful too, as were my explorations of the work and lives of Graham Greene, William Stephenson, William Fairbairn and Roald Dahl.

Shane Peacock is a biographer, journalist, screen-writer and the author of more than a dozen books for young readers, including The Boy Sherlock Holmes series. His work has won many honors, including the Geoffrey Bilson Award, the Libris Award and two Arthur Ellis Awards for Crime Fiction. His novel *Becoming Holmes* was a finalist for the Governor General's Award. Because Shane often writes about unusual subjects, his research methods have, at times, been out of the ordinary too; he has learned tight-rope walking, silent killing, trapeze flying and sumo eating, all in the service of his art. Shane and his wife, journalist Sophie Kneisel, live with their three children on a small farm near Cobourg, Ontario, where he continues to search for and imagine larger-than-life characters. In his spare time he enjoys playing hockey, reading and sometimes even walking the wire. *Double You* is the sequel to *Last Message*, Shane's novel in Seven (the series).